Deadly DELICIOUS

K. L. Kincy

Cover art by Kirbi Fagan

ISBN: 149520622X
ISBN-13: 978-1495206221

DEDICATION

To Chelsea, for poking me to publish this book.

Deadly DELICIOUS

Fall of 1949. Louisiana.

ZERO

I bend over the coffee-dark creek, looking real hard for any magic. The sun slides over the water like a pat of butter on a hot skillet. Supposed to be something extra special underwater, but I'm not seeing anything unusual.

"Conjure's thick here, Josephine." Grandma Lula dabs her sweaty forehead with her handkerchief. "Keep your eyes peeled."

I breathe in slow, in case I can sniff it out. Where the sun hits the thick crust of leaves on mud, a sweet, root-beer smell rises up.

"Grandma?" I say. "What is it we're looking for, again?"

She glances sideways at me. "I suppose you're old enough to know. Somewhere in this swamp, my own grandma lost her grimoire."

"Grimoire?"

"Child, you know what a grimoire is. A magic book, full of all her secret recipes for cooking up conjure. The best witches alive today have got nothing on my grandma. She didn't settle for no small-fry spells."

I sit on a gnarled old log, my toes squishing the muck. "So why'd she lose her grimoire?"

Grandma Lula's nostrils flare. "She tangled with a powerful voodoo spirit by the name of Shaula. Prettier than anything, and twice as deadly. The two of them near killed each other, and the grimoire got lost in this very swamp."

I stare into the water. If there's a book down there, it's got to be rotten mush.

"Josephine," Grandma Lula says, "you're going to be the one to find it. You've got some of the strongest conjure I've felt in ages."

I sigh. She keeps on saying this, no matter how many times I prove her wrong.

She clamps my shoulder with her fingers. "Go on. Use your gift."

"Sure thing," I say, "but only if you watch out for gators."

I wade up to my waist in the creek. Sparkling sun and fluttering leaves fill my mind with commotion, so I shut my eyes so I can think clearer. I spread my palms flat against the water, feeling for any undercurrents of magic.

"Deeper than that," Grandma Lula says, "no doubt

2

about it."

I scrunch up my nose. "It's slimy in here."

"Just a little farther."

I slide my bare feet forward against the cool mud, praying I won't accidentally kick an angry crawdad's claws—or worse, a gator just waiting to chomp up a girl like me. My skin prickles. Are there electric eels in Louisiana?

"Grandma?" I say, my voice wavering. "I—"

Like a bomb went off, a ripple of magic surges through the water, stealing my breath away and knocking me off my feet. I topple backwards into the creek, snorting water up my nose. Darkness closes over my head, and my thrashing stirs up so much mud I can't tell up from down. I kick hard, and my head pops into air.

"You ain't going to drown," Grandma Lula says matter-of-factly.

She marches into the creek herself, latches onto my hand, and drags me out. Coughing, I slump on the bank while she whacks me on the back, knocking water out of my lungs. Stinky mud cakes me head-to-toe.

Grandma Lula bends in front of me, her eyes fierce. "What happened, child?"

"Tripped," I say. "Can we go home now?"

Grandma Lula nods and hauls me to my feet. "That's a crying shame," she mutters.

If I tell her about the magic, she's going to send me

back in after the grimoire. And I'm not sure that's the kind of conjure worth fishing out.

Summer of 1955. Paris, Missouri.

ONE

O nly takes a second for hellfire. One moment I'm flipping burgers, and the next, I'm staggering back from flames whooshing so high they scorch the ceiling. Fire swirls and lashes against the walls, devouring the air. I fall flat on the linoleum, clutching a useless spatula in my fist, and smell my own hair burning.

In the inferno, a face takes shape and leans down over the grill.

"Josephine." It's more sizzle than words, like red-hot steel plunged into water.

Skin of molten orange flame, eyes of hottest blue. I'm a mouse transfixed by a snake. Out of the corner of my eye, I see fire-tentacles crawling toward me.

I roll, lunge to my feet, and twist to grab the fire extinguisher.

The fire-creature sighs in a rush of heat. "I'm coming

for you."

I grit my teeth. "You've got the wrong girl. I ain't even a witch."

I let loose with the fire extinguisher. White sprays over the billowing black smoke, and the fire-creature hisses as it recoils.

Daddy charges into the kitchen, his face as white as his apron. "Josephine!"

"Grease fire!" I shout.

Daddy snatches the fire extinguisher from me and sprays the grill until the flames die to smoke. Coughing, I wilt against a counter. My heart is going about a billion miles an hour. Daddy fixes me with a blue-eyed glare.

I give him an evil look right back. "You abandoned me."

"For two minutes! Two minutes, and you set the kitchen on fire."

"The burgers were getting burnt," I say, in my defense.

"I can see that," he says.

My face flushes. "I wouldn't have touched nothing otherwise."

Daddy's sweating real hard now. He takes off his white paper hat, the one which looks like it belongs on a sailor, and smoothes his damp, dark hair. "*Mon dieu,* it was just flipping burgers," he mutters, his French accent coming out.

Just flipping burgers. Lord almighty.

Maybe if I say it real slow. "I. Can't. Cook."

"*Bien sûr*," Daddy says. Of course.

I square my jaw, my eyes stinging. When I shut my eyes, I can still see that fire-creature, like it burned itself into my eyelids.

"Did you see it, too?" My voice sounds small.

"See what?" Daddy says.

Obviously not. That fire-creature was for my eyes only. I bite the inside of my cheek. This is far from the first time I've crossed paths with weird magic, but usually it makes sense—like shadows dancing in the swamp on full moon nights, or ghosts drifting around the graveyard on Halloween. Nothing much to do with me.

I shrug. "Can I go now?"

"Josephine Elle DeLune." Daddy heaves a big sigh and bundles me into his arms. I squirm away because he's sweaty and I'm not anywhere near a baby anymore. "Hold still. Let me see if you got burned anywhere."

I shake my head. "Just my hair."

He squints at me. "Mama won't even notice." He gives me a meaningful look.

Oh, I have a strong suspicion Mama is going to do more than notice, but I keep my mouth shut and exit through the back door. I sit on the sidewalk and twist my fingers together so they stop shaking. Black smoke rises above Carl and Earl's Drive-In, and quite a few customers have left their cars to point. Big news for our small town.

"Wow, what combusted in there?"

Quentin Cole strolls up, on foot at a drive-in, but then again he can be a rather contrary boy. The quizzical smirk on his face gives me a peculiar feeling, halfway between wanting to smack him and smile back at him.

"Nothing spectacular," I lie through my teeth. "A run-of-the-mill grease fire."

Quentin tries to smooth back his hair, which is the color of corn silk, and that stubborn cowlick above his forehead pokes straight up again. He squints at the smoke, then waves at the ground. "Mind if I join you?" he says.

I roll my eyes. "Quentin, it's just the sidewalk."

"Premium sidewalk! The most comfortable concrete for miles around."

"Is your butt that tender?"

We both stare at each other, then crack up. I'm laughing so hard that I start coughing and wheezing. I rub my aching ribs.

Quentin drapes his arm over my shoulders like he's my brother. "You okay?"

"Think so. Still a lot of smoke in my lungs."

He grimaces. "That's no good."

"That's the third time I near burned down a kitchen."

Quentin's eyebrows go skyward. They're so pale, they're almost invisible. "But your mama is the best cook in Paris."

Make that Paris, Missouri—not the real thing—though

Mama's cooking is amazing.

"Doesn't mean I've got a lick of her talent," I say.

Or, for that matter, a lick of conjure. Never mind that generations of women in my family have magic in their blood, and never mind that Grandma Lula spent years trying to wring it out of me like I was soaked in raw promise. Which makes the fire-creature all the more unusual. Maybe it mistook me for a real witch.

Quentin smiles, his eyes so heavenly blue that I would crumble if I were a lesser girl. "Well, I think you're talented."

"At what?"

"Being a good friend."

I pretend to punch him on the arm. "That's the most disgustingly sweet thing to say."

He shrugs, his cheeks pink. "It's the solemn truth."

By now, most of the smoke from the grease fire has drifted away. The big neon sign buzzes to life above Carl and Earl's, glowing against a sweet blackberry-juice sky, and the crickets begin fiddling in the shadow of the magnolias.

"We could," Quentin says, "make lemonade out of lemons."

I study the way the fireflies float like cinders above the grass. "And how do you propose to do that, Mr. Cole?"

"We have time to catch the matinee for Marooned in the Universe."

My breath sticks in my throat, but I put on a smile. Going to the movies together has been our tradition ever since I first moved to Paris. Trouble is, lately it's been real hard to sit so close to him in the dark. I get this twisted-up squirming feeling inside, like an earthworm tangled with a Slinky. I don't know why, for certain.

"I don't know," I say, "my allowance is looking pretty piddly."

He puffs up his chest and puts on a pompous accent, like an English lord. "Josephine," he says, "in order to be a great actress, one must to study the greats."

I snort. "What do you know about acting? You want to be a director."

"I'd rather be the brains behind a movie, not the beauty."

"Afraid you aren't handsome enough to be on the other side of the camera?" I tease.

"Oh, I don't stand a chance." A strange shadow darkens his eyes. "Next to you."

My smile slips away. There goes that earthworm-Slinky feeling again.

His voice falls to a whisper. "But that's just my opinion."

Oh, lord, oh, sweet Jesus. Is he saying what I think he's saying? My ribs tighten until my heart hurts, and I can't talk for fear of my voice squeaking. Quentin lowers his gaze, his long eyelashes shading his eyes. I fan myself with my hand, a little light-headed. If I faint, is he going to catch me? Of course he would. If he likes me, he isn't going to let me fall. He's going to clutch me in his strong arms and everything's going to go blurry while he leans in close... I grip the sidewalk to keep myself steady.

Then Quentin looks up to me, at my face—no, behind me.

"Quentin!" An airy voice singsongs across the parking lot. "Quentin Cole, is that you?"

My hands clench into fists. Authelia McArthur.

She trips across the lot in sandals, her white sundress rippling in the wind, her hand holding her straw hat over her golden blonde hair. Her lips bend into a pretty little smile, and she lowers her sunglasses to peer at us.

"Oh," she says, breathily of course, "am I interrupting something?"

"Well," I say, "we—"

"No," Quentin says, smiling politely, his eyes on Authelia now.

Authelia's smile shows a little bit of teeth. She just eats it up when boys stare at her.

I clear my throat. "What brings you here?"

"Everybody for ten miles can see that smoke. And where there's smoke, there's fire." Her gaze settles on Quentin, for some reason.

"Sorry to disappoint," I say, "but there are no handsome firefighters coming."

Authelia squints at me like I'm dog poop on her shoe. "Did you burn your eyebrows?"

"Probably." I stare coolly at her. "At least I didn't pluck them to death."

"I'm sure you could afford a pair of tweezers."

I grin with clenched teeth. "Are you wearing lipstick? And here I thought your mama forbid makeup until you turned sixteen."

Authelia just laughs and shakes her head. "Oh, Josephine. You're so hilarious."

I hate how she's daring to call me by name, like she still has any right to.

Quentin, still Mr. Picture of Politeness, says, "How are things going, Authelia?"

"Mother's at a charity auction," Authelia says, "and Father's still at work. I decided to go for a walk, since I was feeling sort of lonely."

Lonely? She has a lot of nerve, saying that in front of my face. But I bite my tongue.

"Father's super busy because we're having such a hard time meeting demand over at McArthur Mills." She titters, one hand over her mouth. "Josephine, has your mama been doing a lot of extra baking lately?"

I don't bother telling her that Mama would never let such inferior flour in her kitchen.

"I meant," Quentin says, "how are you?"

Quentin! For once in your life, you don't have to be

nice to everybody.

"Oh, great!" Authelia chirps. "Just great... I was thinking about the movies tonight."

Quentin perks up. "We were just going to see Marooned in the Universe. You want to come with us?"

I try real hard not to let my face twist with disgust.

Authelia's face sours. "Us?"

He appears to have absolutely no clue. "Yeah, you're welcome to—"

"I'm not going," I say.

"Oh." Quentin looks puzzled. "Okay."

Authelia leans forward and makes her voice even breathier, if that's at all possible. "Would you like to take me, instead?"

A shy grin steals over Quentin's face. "Sure!"

I feel like I'm going to puke. "Fantastic," I mutter.

I climb to my feet and wave goodbye to Quentin, but he's not even paying attention to me now. I could *punch* him goodbye, and he probably wouldn't notice until tomorrow. He staring at Authelia with this happy dumb look in his eyes. My stomach somersaults as I hop onto my bicycle, and I taste bitterness in my mouth.

I've been betrayed in favor of Authelia McArthur.

***

I pedal hard on the way home, the cool evening air

rushing into my stinging eyes. A clump of my curly black hair whips into my face, and I yank it behind my ear until it behaves. Nothing like Authelia's silky blonde hair, or her magnolia-petal skin. *She* could be in Hollywood, if she only tried.

My skin is more coffee than cream, just like Mama's, but my hair isn't nearly as smooth or as straight as hers. Authelia used to give me this pitying pout and call my curls "exotic," which would send Mama after my hair like an avenging fury with a Lustrasilk home permanent kit. Heaven forbid I look uncivilized.

"Authelia, Authelia, Authelia." Just saying her name makes my blood boil.

Believe me, she wasn't always that kind of girl. Sure, she was blonde and breathy-voiced since the day she was born, but she didn't act so stupid until her thirteenth birthday party. It was like aliens beamed out her brain and added a new one addicted to kissing boys and gossiping about every nasty secret in school—though it probably wasn't aliens, just the popular girls at school. She actually *invited* them, and ignored everybody else.

How do I know all this? Did I mention we used to be best friends?

Mama will talk me to death if I'm late for supper, so I take the shortcut through the swamp. Cypress trees swoon over a pond so choked with duckweed you can't even see water. A bullfrog croaks all by its lonesome. Mosquitoes whine in the muggy soup of air, spurring me to go faster, but the bumpy road rattles my bicycle so bad that I get off and walk. No point in coming to the table covered in swamp scum.

Wind hisses through the cattails, and the tiny hairs on my arms stand at attention. Shivering, I hug myself tight and squint in the growing gloom. I just felt... power. A great murmur of magic flowing out from the darkness. Did that fire-creature spark back to life? But the swamp is one of the wettest places around, and—

Duckweed ripples, and a woman rises from the water.

Her skin gleams black, true black, sparkling with pinpricks of light—like stars in the night sky. Her dripping wet hair, as thick and wild as brambles, twists past her waterlogged white dress. Her eyes are dark, without any white in them. She doesn't look even partway real, despite the droplets trickling down her face.

She smiles at me. She's scary gorgeous.

Then she pulls up a fistful of rotting blonde hair, and the body of Authelia McArthur.

"This what you wanted?" the night-skinned lady asks, in a New Orleans accent.

One look at empty eyes and cold white skin and I'm back on my bike and pedaling like the Devil himself is after me—and he might be, at this rate. Mud splatters my legs as I hightail it out of the swamp. There's no way I'm going to let myself get strangled by a crazy woman and rot in the swamp next to Authelia.

When I glance back, gasping for breath, the night-skinned lady and the body are gone.

Last time I felt magic like that was also in a swamp. Back in Louisiana, when I was eight years old. Grandma Lula wanted me to fish out a magic cookbook, a grimoire by my great-great-grandma... a grimoire she lost in a battle of conjure.

She tangled with a powerful voodoo spirit by the name of Shaula. Prettier than anything, and twice as deadly.

I have an awful suspicion Shaula is back.

TWO

I park my bicycle beneath the Osage orange tree by our creaky-boned townhouse, which is older than all of us DeLunes put together, trip over one of the green fruits, and swear under my breath. I'm not too happy about the hurt in my stubbed toe, which kind of proves that I'm not dreaming.

First the fire-creature, then the night-skinned lady who might be Shaula. What did I do to deserve this much crazy in one day? Maybe I blundered into somebody else's magical business, and everybody will leave me alone once they realize I'm a dud, about as great as a flat soufflé. Some other witch can take care of this voodoo.

I should tell Mama. She knows gobs more about conjure than I do.

Through the screen door, the vanilla-sweet scent of baking floats into the evening. I suck in air real slow, the tightness in my muscles relaxing.

I bound up the crooked stairs and slip into the kitchen. "Mama?" I call.

No reply.

Cooling on top of Mama's prized pink appliances, her secret-recipe DeLune DeLuxe doughnuts perfume the air with the aromas of happiness, confidence, and good luck. My head gets all whirly as I breathe in deep.

These doughnuts are pretty enough to be hanging on a Christmas tree. They're all twinkly with sprinkles, and plump enough that I'm just itching to squeeze them. Oh, look, chocolate filling leaking from the good luck doughnut. I glance around the kitchen. The coast's clear, so I dip my pinkie into the chocolate.

A stinging blow lands on my knuckles. Mama's choice walnut-wood spatula.

Even though she can't actually poof from a cloud of smoke, it still scares the bejesus out of me when she pounces like that. She's wearing her favorite coral pink suit and pillbox hat, her hair all glossy—she must have just drove up.

"For customers only," Mama says.

Like I don't have any wishes of my own. I wonder who gets to devour these DeLune DeLuxe doughnuts—could be anybody, really, except the Stewarts, who live way up on that hill, don't let their kids play with nobody, and don't trust food that's a little too good to be true. Around here,

Mama's cooking is the secret everybody knows, but nobody dares admit that conjure is the secret ingredient. Witchcraft and voodoo are most certainly not topics of polite conversation in Paris.

Paying no mind to Mama's flared nostrils, I lick my pinkie clean.

"Josephine," she says, "you smell like smoke. What happened to your hair?"

"Singed it," I say. "We had a grease fire today."

"Good lord!" Mama plants her hand on her hip in that no-nonsense-I'm-going-to-lecture-you way. "That's what your daddy calls waitressing?"

"I'm not a waitress," I say. "I'm a carhop-in-training."

"Honey, running around on rollerskates isn't the only way to earn your allowance."

This is only the hundredth time she's dragged out that argument. "Mama."

"According to your daddy, you spend an awful lot of time *carhopping* for that Cole boy."

"Mama!" My stomach does a weird lurch, like an elevator going down. "We're friends."

She fixes me with a stare. "You are twelve years old, Josephine. You are growing far too mature to be nothing more than a friends with a boy."

My face always gets annoyingly hot when I argue. "How do you know?"

Mama's eyes narrow. "Don't you talk back to me,

Josephine DeLune."

I throw up my hands like she's holding a gun. "I'm not!"

"Your future ain't in fast food, honey." She presses her hand to her bosom. "My very own daughter, turning her back on conjure."

I almost laugh. Conjure turned its back on me.

"You should be standing beside me in the kitchen," she says. "It's your birthright."

"I'll think about it," I say in a flat voice.

She sighs and starts fussing with my curls. "As for your singed hair, it's about time you had a haircut. And some Lustrasilk."

I grimace. "No, thanks. I'll just be more careful around open flames."

She shakes her head and walks away, her sensible heels clicking on the linoleum. "Get ready for supper. I just need to pop it in the oven."

"Yes, Mama."

I heave a sigh. Now is not the time to tell her about the fire-creature or the night-skinned lady. She's going to think I'm not a failure in all things conjure, and she's only going to try twice as hard to force me into a life of witchcraft.

I wish I could tell her the truth, and that she would understand.

Heck, who said conjure was all that great, anyway?

Obviously it hasn't gotten Mama anywhere but working from dawn to dusk baking magic for rich folks like Authelia. Daddy makes as much money from plain old fast food. I hear them arguing about it in the kitchen sometimes, when I'm supposed to be sleeping. We're pretty close to poorer than dirt, and certainly get stepped on just about as much.

Swallowing my words, I climb upstairs to my attic bedroom, which is so sweltering hot I feel about ready to faint. I fling all the windows open, kick off my shoes, and peel away my carhop uniform. I scrub my face and hands, then drag on a dress respectable enough for supper. There's nothing I can do about my hair, which stinks like smoke, fried potatoes, fried chicken, fried catfish, fried everything.

I flop on my bed and gaze at the poster of Amandine LeClair hanging over my pillow. She smiles at me, her lips fire-engine red, the same color as her silky gown. Her hair ripples in gentle auburn waves. Absolutely gorgeous. If Amandine bottled up her glamour like a perfume, I'd wear it every day. She grew up in some backwater little French village, and now she's plenty rich and famous. One of these days, I'm going to find my destiny in Hollywood. If I were a star, I'd never want anything I couldn't have.

Just thinking about it gives me a special feeling of satisfaction. Conjure can't do that.

Outside, twilight slips into purple night, and when I let

my hair down and lean out the window, I feel like Rapunzel. Only, fairy tale princesses are supposed to be blonde like Authelia, and I'm not too keen on being rescued by a prince. Could Quentin be my prince? I think of him riding a big white horse, and laugh.

"Josephine!"

Down on the sidewalk, Cleon waves at me, then glances over his shoulder and blows a kiss to a pretty poodle-skirted girl, who blushes. I roll my eyes. Another sweetheart? He's only three years older than me, but he's a regular Romeo, always tangled up in some romance or another. Some people have all the luck, doughnuts or no doughnuts.

"What's for supper?" Cleon yells to me.

"I don't know," I yell back. "Ask Mama."

"Stop hollering, you two!" Mama leans out of the kitchen window. "You're going to disturb the neighbors! Besides, it's suppertime."

Cleon sniffs the air. "Nutrition detected. Analysis complete... eggs? Bacon?"

Mama flaps a dishtowel at him. "If you keep up with that astronaut talk, you're eating nothing but space food for a week."

She's smiling, though, because Cleon's brains make her proud. Unlike me, the rebel DeLune, he does what Mama and Daddy tell him to, studies real hard, and has his sights set on a school big enough for his scientist dreams.

See, Cleon's a boy. He has no business in the world of witchcraft.

Right after Mama pops inside, Daddy drives up in his pumpkin-colored pickup truck. He honks at us, and we wave back. I try to catch his eye, to warn him what Mama's about to dish out, but he's too busy backing into the driveway.

I'm not very hungry anymore, but not eating Mama's cooking is tantamount to suicide. Either she nags you to pieces, or decides you must be sick and stuffs you with "healing" conjure that tastes like a puree of dog poo and swamp scum. Nasty. She has the talent to make anything taste good, so I doubt it's by accident.

Sometimes you just can't win with Mama.

I run downstairs and almost crash into Cleon, but the two of us have straightened out our clothes and are sitting ramrod straight at the table by the time Mama comes in with a casserole dish between her pink oven mitts.

Cleon and I both crane our necks to get a better look. A flaky golden crust with a soft white filling, browned gently on top, sprinkled with melted cheese and squares of ham. The scent of eggs, cheese, and just a hint of garlic steams to our noses.

"What is it?" I breathe.

Mama smiles a big smile. "Quiche Lorraine, from the real Paris."

"That's from France?" Cleon says, with his trademark

crooked smile.

"The recipe, yes," she says. "A DeLune original."

Daddy saunters in and plants a kiss on Mama's lips without waiting for her to put down the casserole. "You're married to the DeLune original."

Cleon rolls his eyes at me.

"Laurent," Mama says, her voice even. "Wash up for supper."

Smiling, Daddy heads into the kitchen. Mama shoots a dirty look at the back of his head, and I sink lower in my chair. Cleon raises his eyebrows at me, and I shrug. He's going to find out soon enough why Mama's so mad.

Daddy strolls back inside, drying his hands on his jeans.

"So is the quiche Lorraine recipe from Grand-mère and Grand-père?" I say brightly, trying to avoid the storm brewing in the room.

"*Oui*," Daddy says. "One of the most popular dishes at their restaurant, before the war."

Cleon cocks his head. "Looks like a pie full of scrambled eggs and ham."

"Wait until you taste it," Daddy says.

"I tweaked the recipe a bit," Mama says. "Bespelled with a bit of clarity and foresight."

She always adds a dollop of conjure for truly enchanting cuisine. I hold out my plate for the first slice, my tongue already aching for a taste.

"Which," she adds, "you look like you could use,

Laurent."

Daddy sputters on the water he'd been drinking. "Excuse me?"

Mama's eyes gleam as she serves me a slice of quiche. "Josephine came home today with quite a story to tell. Don't you think?"

"Did she?" Daddy says, with a sharp look at me.

I take a bite of the quiche, so I have an excuse not to talk. It is, of course, delicious, but then Mama's cooking rarely isn't.

"Clara," Daddy says. "No one was hurt."

"They could have been." Mama sets down Cleon's plate a little too hard. "I don't like the idea of Josephine playing around at the drive-in."

Lord, I'm not a kindergartener!

"Playing around?" Daddy raises his eyebrows. "She's helping the family business."

"*The* family business?" Mama says.

"Of course not." He smiles. "Burgers *and* baking are the DeLune business."

Mama sighs as dramatically as any movie star damsel. "Sometimes I wonder why I married a Frenchman with such bad taste in food."

Daddy clutches his ribs and slumps. "A mortal wound to my culinary pride."

A smile creeps across Mama's face. "You know I'm only teasing, Laurent." She swats playfully at his hand. "Finish your quiche."

We all exhale and keep eating. By the end of supper, there's only a sliver of a slice left.

"I'm still hungry," Cleon says, with a longing glance at the quiche.

"You know better than that." Mama moves the slice onto a tiny silver plate. "Josephine, it's time to give Papa Nom his supper."

I nod, even though I really don't care.

Together, we head out to the backyard. Under the oldest, most twisted magnolia tree, there's a little stone table. Our statue of Papa Nom sits on top, a doughy-fat man made of clay. He cradles his big belly with pudgy fingers, his mouth frozen in a grin, his eyes nothing more than holes poked into clay by some witch a long time ago.

Mama places the silver plate before Papa Nom, then uncorks a bottle of rum. "Thank you, Papa Nom, for blessing our food and giving us empty bellies to fill. Amen." She pours a shot glass of rum, then drizzles half of it over Papa Nom.

Kind of a waste of quiche, if you ask me. Some possum is just going to eat it.

"Josephine?" Mama holds out the rest of the rum to me.

Even though I'm not a practicing witch, I've got conjure in my blood, and she swears that I'll insult Papa Nom if I don't offer to him, too.

I take the rum and pour it over Papa Nom. It trickles down his smiling face. "Amen."

Does it matter if you say it, but don't believe it?

Mama smiles at me and squeezes my arm, and I know she's trying to say sorry for our quarrel. I squeeze her hand back.

***

I lie in bed, my thoughts swimming in my head like a goldfish in a too-small bowl. The fire-creature at Carl and Earl's... Authelia snatching Quentin out from under my nose... the night-skinned lady dragging around Authelia's body...

This what you wanted?

No. That's not me. Cross my heart, I don't mean to hurt Authelia. I just want her to wake up and turn back into my friend. She thinks she belongs with the popular girls—the nasty ones—but she's not one of them. Not really.

I blow out my breath in a hiss and roll over in bed, dragging the blankets over my head.

When I shut my eyes, I'm standing in the swamp again. Hip-deep in the water, I wade past slimy things I can't see, though I can certainly imagine all manner of eels and leeches. Goosebumps dot my arms. A laugh slithers through the blackness; when the fog tatters, I see someone standing on the grass above me.

The night-skinned lady.

Instead of dragging Authelia around like a doll, this time she's standing real close to Quentin—*kissing* him. Her arms snake round his shoulders. Heat scorches my face, and I'm the most guilty peeping tom in the universe.

"You like him." Her voice sounds like a river of honey. "Don't you?"

I shake my head. "Sorry, ma'am, but you must be mistaken."

She arches an eyebrow, and Quentin vanishes from her arms, no more than mist. "There's no use in trying to fool me, *ma chère*."

"I'm not a witch. I can't cook. Honest to goodness, I want to be an actress."

"You're wrong." She just plain says it. "All you need is a good recipe, Miss DeLune."

"You're wasting your time."

"Time is one thing you have very little of." The night-skinned lady steps toward me, offering her hand, but I'm a little preoccupied staring at her feet—not feet at all, but cloven hooves. Like the Devil. "You are being hunted."

I retreat from the voodoo spirit. "By who? You?"

"Of course not."

"I'm not stupid. Why should I trust you?"

She stares at me. "I'm your only hope of help."

When I look into her black eyes for too long, my legs lock up and my head swirls, like I'm leaning over the edge of a cliff.

"I know who you are," I say. "Shaula."

"Yes," she says. Her outline starts drifting apart like ink in water.

I clench my hands into fists and do what I always do when I want to wake up from a bad dream: blink and blink until my eyes open. "You tried to kill my great-great-grandma. You probably want to kill me, too. I've got her blood in my veins, after all."

Shaula half-frowns, half-smiles. "I can see..."

A wind blows away the rest of her words, but I catch the very last bit.

"...family."

I jolt upright in bed, my nightie dripping wet like I fell into the swamp, only it's sweat.

Shaula.

The voodoo spirit who fought my great-great-grandma, who was by all accounts a powerful witch, is here for me, and I am by all accounts powerless indeed.

A book has fallen straight from the bookcase onto my bed, lying between my knees. A dog-eared dictionary, the faded old pages open to the D's. And in the edges of the entry for Delicious, there's a scribbled note. I fumble to turn on the lamp.

Win Quentin.

In my handwriting. I slide my finger over the words, and the ink smudges.

I don't write in books, never have. When Cleon and I were babies, Mama made us swear we wouldn't ruin them. And I most definitely wouldn't be writing down sappy daydreams like some girls do. Or even having daydreams about Quentin in the first place. Would I? Lord, I don't even know anymore. Did Shaula make me write this?

Needless to say, I've got a real problem if a voodoo spirit is possessing me in my sleep.

A breeze sighs through my open window and ruffles the pages. When they settle down, I lean forward. Still in the D's, but farther along alphabetically speaking. There's a drawing, the likes of which I've never seen, scribbled over a whole page of words—a black tangle of squiggles that seems to have no rhyme or reason to it. In the middle of the tangle, though, if I stare real hard, there's what looks like a round mouth ringed with teeth.

The word above this drawing: *Devourer.*

A shudder ripples down my spine. I slam the dictionary shut, jump out of bed, and tiptoe downstairs to the kitchen. I open the back door slowly so it doesn't squeal, then creep outside in nothing but my nightie and dump the dictionary into the garbage can. The cursed thing tumbles onto broken eggshells and coffee grounds.

"Enough is enough," I whisper.

"Josephine?"

I freeze. Daddy flicks on the light. He's standing in the doorway in his pajamas, a doughnut in his hand—one of

Mama's doughnuts.

"What are you doing?" he says.

"What are *you* doing?" I say right back.

He looks at the doughnut in his hand. "Midnight snack."

"I won't tell Mama if you don't."

He laughs, but his eyebrows look worried. "Something wrong, Jo?"

"I'm just glad I'm a fast-food kind of girl, and not a witchy one."

"You think?" Daddy says.

Of course that doesn't help me feel any less afraid.

THREE

As Mama serves up omelets for breakfast, Daddy leans back in his chair, pats his stomach, and sighs contemplatively.

Mama cracks an egg onto the griddle, where it sizzles. "What is it, Laurent?"

"It's about that time of year at Carl and Earl's," he says, "to start cooking our limited-time super-special giant onion rings."

Limited-time super-special giant onion rings? My favorite! They're even crispier and crunchier than the ones you can get at the state fair.

"With secret sauce?" I ask.

Daddy winks. "Of course."

"Secret sauce?" Mama rolls her eyes as she flips another omelet.

"Not another word," Daddy teases. "It's confidential."

Mama starts to say something, but he kisses her in mid-sentence. She smiles and pretends to swat him with her spatula.

"Don't taste-test too many onion rings before supper," she says.

Daddy laughs. "Wouldn't dream of it." He grabs his coat and heads for the door.

Cleon coughs and buries his nose deeper in his book. The cover shows a rocket landing on the moon, so I'm guessing his brain is in outer space right now.

"You two done with omelets?" Mama says. "I have some baking to get started."

"I'm full, thanks." Cleon bookworms his way upstairs.

"Don't trip and break your ankle!" Mama says. "Lord, one of these days…"

I poke at the onions in my omelet. I don't know if I should be setting foot in Carl and Earl's after the whole fire-creature incident. An ugly, lopsided feeling crawls around inside my stomach, like I ate something alive.

Time is one thing you have very little of.

"Any plans today, Josephine?" Mama says, oh-so-innocently.

Uh-oh. She wants me to help in the kitchen. Remedial stove skills, or something.

"Hanging out with friends," I say real quick. "It's a nice day."

Mama squints out the window. Curdled-milk clouds

spill across the sky; birds and bugs fly so low their bellies almost scrape dirt.

"Rain's coming, if you ask me," Mama says. "Wear your jacket."

I scarf down the rest of my omelet and swig some orange juice. "I will."

"You sure you don't want—?"

"Nope!"

Her little league conjure isn't going to help me today.

I'm not dumb enough to shortcut through the swamp again, so I bike the long way to Carl and Earl's. Of course, this means passing the McArthur mansion, a big wedding cake of a house. Luckily, it doesn't look like Authelia is home. A scattering of peacocks struts around their emerald velvet lawn, pecking and scratching at the grass like overdressed chickens. I don't recognize the turquoise Buick in the circle driveway, but then again the McArthurs buy new cars like regular folks buy bubblegum.

It doesn't seem all that long ago that I walked up their driveway with a plate of Mama's cookies. Authelia answered the door, nothing more than a pale little girl, and blinked at me like I was a mirage. When she gave me a tour of her house, I couldn't stop gawking at the kitchen's granite counters, the den's leather couches, the dining room's Swarovski chandeliers—heck, back then I thought Swarovski was a kind of diamond.

I grit my teeth and start pedaling again. I don't want

Authelia to see me standing here outside her house like Oliver Twist waiting for some more gruel. Heavens, I'm not that pitiful, and I'm not the sort of girl who pines.

An eerily cheerful song echoes off some houses behind me. I glance back.

A vanilla-white ice cream truck drives behind me, playing, "Twinkle, Twinkle, Little Star." The driver isn't from around here. He's a pop-eyed black man with a wide mouth and drooping mustache, like a catfish wriggling across a flooded field. He waves at me. I wave back, kind of feebly, and pedal harder. Don't know why he's playing tunes on a day like this, when nobody would possibly want anything cold to eat.

You are being hunted.

No, I'm pretty sure Shaula wasn't talking about an ice cream truck man. More along the lines of that black tangle with teeth under Devourer in my dictionary. But it's not like I've ever seen one of those strolling the streets of Paris.

First thing I notice at Carl and Earl's: there's a line of cars long enough to stretch to the moon and back, complete with honking horns and angry customers. Next thing I notice: Gordon, the biggest, meanest fry cook in existence, barges around the kitchen like an angry walrus, his cigarette dangling from his lip.

"Excuse me!" I call. I tack on a, "Sir!" just to be safe.

Gordon squints at me. "You got my onions?"

"No," I say. "I'm looking for my daddy."

Gordon chomps on his cigarette. "Hell's bells, we don't need no little girls poking around this establishment. We need onions!"

"Don't panic," Daddy says, stepping into the kitchen. "They're coming."

I raise my eyebrows. "You're out of onion rings already?"

"Sorry, Jo." Daddy gives me a frazzled smile. "No taste-testing."

"I can help," I say. "With the orders and stuff."

Daddy tosses me an apron. "Go for it."

I grab my skates from their cubby. As soon as I tie a knot in my apron strings and stand up straight, I feel taller. I whiz out of there like a pro, just as fast as the other carhops—the *real* carhops. Two of them flag me down, their ponytails bobbing, their perfect mascara not even smudged in the summer heat.

"You're in for a real doozy today," Lauralee says.

"Good luck!" Shirley says.

"I'd better get to work," I say, more to myself than anyone else.

Goodness, this does look like a doozy of a day. Customers keep rapping their fingers on their steering wheels, no matter how much I say I'm sorry for the wait. I'm scribbling down orders so fast my pencil is close to catching fire.

"Three extra large cheeseburgers, three sides of curly fries, and three coca-colas."

"A burger. No bun. Yes, miss, just a burger. Oh, and could you throw in a pickle?"

"You'ns got any of those fried catfish here?"

"Things would go a little faster if people weren't so damn lazy."

That last comment gets muttered behind my back, and I wheel around in time to see Floyd Glumphy's sour face behind his nasty old brown Chevrolet, which is held together by bits of rust and prayer on his part, no doubt.

I grit my teeth. Wonderful.

Word is, Mr. Glumphy was born crotchety. His own mama tried to donate him to the hospital when he was a baby, and it went downhill from there. He couldn't get any job except for postmaster, which he hates so much people drive to other zip codes just to buy stamps. Myself included, since he especially hates young folks.

I hear happy twinkling music, followed by the ice cream truck itself. The driver shuts off his music and pulls into line. By the time I get to him, I brace myself for yet another cranky customer, but he gives me an unsettling smile.

"Can I take your order, sir?" I say.

"Sir?" His laugh is as dark and rich as chocolate. "Call me Aloysius. And you are?"

"Josephine."

"Josephine..." He says my name like he's tasting it. "Mmm-hmm. You look real familiar. Have we met?"

"Can't say we have."

"I'm sure I've seen hair as lovely as yours somewhere before."

Lord, maybe I really should succumb to Lustrasilk. These curls are nothing but trouble.

"Why, thank you." I fake a smile. "Sorry, sir, but I really better take your order before there's too much of a backlog."

"All right," Aloysius says. "I'll have your curly fries and a double-decker burger."

"Yes, sir. Right away."

I skate off to grab Mr. Glumphy's orange shake and cheeseburger, no pickle, no mustard, extra onions. I'd add some spit, if I was that sort of girl. He's still sour-faced when I deliver it to him, and he takes his burger apart and stares at the pieces.

What's his problem? A corncob stuck up his butt? I try not to roll my eyes as I leave.

"Hope this burger doesn't have no witchery in it," he mutters behind my back.

My stomach sours, and I have to stop myself from wobbling on my skates. I wheel back around. "Excuse me?" I say, my voice sweet.

Mr. Glumphy's fingers clamp around the burger. "Hope this is fresh."

"Why, yes, sir," I say. "Extra fresh. Unless you'd like to ask the cook himself."

"Don't bother." He scowls and chomps on his burger. "I trust *his* cooking."

But not me delivering it, since I'm a maybe-witchy girl.

Cheeks blazing, I speed away. A pink-and-white Cadillac pulls into the drive-in, and I just about crash. Authelia blabs in the back seat, flipping her blonde ponytail over her shoulder, while next to her some teenage girl I don't know fakes a breathless giggle and plumps up her curls. They're chauffeured by Mrs. McArthur, all dolled up in a perfect flamingo-pink sundress, white gloves, and a straw hat trimmed with roses. Mrs. McArthur looks like a clone of her daughter, only droopier, and with more makeup.

Of course I have to take their order, but I can do it with a minimum of niceness.

"Welcome to Carl and Earl's what do you want today?" I say it all in one breath.

Mrs. McArthur arches one eyebrow and lowers her cat's eye sunglasses. "Hello." Just that one word drips with more venom than a nest of cottonmouths. "Honey, are you still working here?" She says 'working' like it's a dirty word.

My face blazes. "I'm helping the family business," I say through a clenched-teeth grin.

"How horrible," Authelia says.

"How old are you, honey?" Mrs. McArthur says, her voice dripping pity. "Ten?"

Either she forgot how old I am, or she can't count.

"Twelve," I say.

Mrs. McArthur clucks. "Honey, there are laws against this sort of thing."

If she calls me 'honey' one more time...

"I'm helping my daddy," I say. "I'm not getting paid."

"Honestly." Authelia snickers. "I wouldn't *want* to work for free."

"Authelia, darling," her mother says, with a glance in her rearview mirror, "let's not be unkind to people less fortunate than ourselves."

"Well, it's basically *slave labor*," Authelia whispers loudly to her friend.

Her friend looks scandalized, her stare all over my skin.

I make my voice loud and perky. "What will your order be?"

Ms. McArthur fakes a smile. "Girls, what do you want?"

Authelia tosses her hair. "We'd like your double-decker cheeseburgers, jumbo curly fries, strawberry lemonade—"

"I don't like strawberry lemonade," says her friend, in a mousy voice.

"But Edna," Authelia simpers, "you know it's my favorite."

The girl slumps back in her seat, her thin shoulders drooping.

"Strawberry lemonade," Authelia says, "corn dogs, and coca-colas. Two of everything. Are you getting all that, or am I talking too fast?"

I grip my pencil so hard it digs a hole in my paper. "Got it."

"I'll have a Caesar salad," Mrs. McArthur says.

"Sorry, we don't serve that here. Ma'am. There's coleslaw?"

She sighs and checks her pastel pink lipstick in a mirror. "A side of fries. That's all."

As I skate away, I hear Edna mutter, "Is she really twelve?"

"What do you think?" Authelia says airily. "They can't afford another carhop."

Edna forces a bright laugh.

I grit my teeth. They can't possibly eat all that food at once; they must have ordered so much out of charity. I hate how Edna just sits there drooping. She's obviously not one of Authelia's popular friends. She must be a wannabe. I guess Authelia gets her kicks from feeling like a princess with her very own pauper.

I load up my tray with burgers and shakes, then make some more deliveries. "Have a fantastic lunch!" I sing. "The ketchup is great today!" Now I'm grinning like a taxidermied gator. "Hope you enjoy your onion rings!"

Maybe I should tone it down, because the customers are starting to look a little scared.

I'm sorely tempted to put something nasty in Authelia's order—if only I knew some on-the-spot conjure!—but I deliver all that food, even though it's about to be wasted, to their Cadillac with a smile as fake as Edna's giggling.

"Your order," I say, but they're not listening.

"And then," Authelia says, "he stared into my eyes—deeply, you know, as they say—and I knew he was dying to kiss me right then and there, but the poor boy was too shy. So I leaned in close to help him out a little, and our lips met, and..." She sighs as if the rest is simply too fantastic to be put into words.

Mrs. McArthur gives her daughter a soppy look. "Shy, but rather charming."

My wrists are starting to hurt from holding so much food. "Excuse me," I say.

"Oh, that's so romantic!" Edna sighs.

Authelia smiles. "Quentin thought so, too."

My heart stops.

"He could hardly contain himself," she goes on, "but I bid him goodnight."

She has to be lying. Quentin would never kiss her.

Authelia shoots me a nasty glare. "Were you eavesdropping, Josephine?"

"I have better things to do." I shove the platter at her. "Here's your food."

"Josephine!" she squeals.

Ms. McArthur glares at me over her sunglasses. "Don't

spill anything on the upholstery."

I blush. "I wasn't."

"Honey," she says, "you should work on your customer service."

Authelia rolls her eyes. "Honestly, Mother, I'm not sure she knows what that is."

Shut up, Authelia, and eat your damn food.

Out loud, I say, "Have a nice day."

Then I skate away before I slap her across the mouth. If I didn't have Daddy to worry about, I would. Instead, I have to listen to her laugh.

"Wow, Authelia, she *was* awful," Edna says, and I hate her, too.

Because I used to be that girl. Authelia's friend.

***

There's no satisfaction in helping customers, or seeing Daddy smile. After awhile, I hang up my apron, and twist my face into a frown when Daddy pokes a fresh-fried onion ring in my face. It doesn't even smell tasty anymore.

"You feeling all right, Jo?" Daddy says.

I shake my head. "Tired. And sick."

I'm really sick and tired of awful people, but I don't tell him that.

"You want a ride home?"

"Sure."

Daddy hoists my bike into the back of the pickup truck, and we rattle along the roads toward home. The sun slides down the sky like an egg yolk in a purple bowl. It would be pretty if I didn't have such ugly thoughts inside.

"Daddy?" I say. "Am I too young to help at Carl and Earl's?"

"Why?" Daddy looks sideways at me. "When I was your age in Paris, I learned how to cook with Grand-mère and Grand-père."

"In their restaurant?"

"*Oui*, in their restaurant. I cook differently now, but I learned a lot."

Well, that's France.

When we get home, Mama isn't even working on supper. She's busy measuring spices and dumping them into a bowl of what smells like lemon juice, a determined glint in her eyes. A bottle of half-gone rum stands beside her. The radio's on with the sound down low, playing the antsy rhythm of "Rock Around the Clock."

"We're home!" Daddy calls. "I'm going to take a shower before supper."

Mama nods absently and blows him a kiss.

I stand in the door, blinking owlishly. "What're you making?"

"Pie," she says.

"For dessert?"

Mama snorts. "Not unless you want to fall head over

heels for some stranger."

Oh. She's making strawberry-rhubarb Sweetheart Pie, a difficult creation not often ordered. One of her priciest recipes, too. If she can pull this one off, we won't have to worry about groceries for maybe a month.

"Rhubarb needs to be marinated for three whole days," Mama says, like I'm her student.

I nod, and my stomach rumbles. "What's for supper?"

"Pasta salad. In the fridge. Don't you even think about stealing a bite until I'm done with this." Mama raises her voice. "Cleon!"

My brother runs downstairs, no doubt just as hungry. "What, Mama?"

"Start setting the table with Josephine."

Mama corks a jar and sweeps over to her spice cabinet. Her sleeve knocks a piece of paper off the counter, which flutters to the floor by my feet.

A gift for Quentin Cole.

Somebody ordered him a Sweetheart Pie.

I pick up the paper, my guts tying themselves into knots. That curly cursive handwriting... I know who it belongs to. Authelia.

***

Supper sits like a cold lump of concrete in my stomach. I lie spread-eagled in bed, my eyes closed, and picture

Quentin smiling and petting Authelia's blonde hair while she laughs her stupid airy laugh. They can both go on some sappy date and feed each other slices of strawberry-rhubarb Sweetheart Pie with their forks.

Just think, they would have never met if I hadn't introduced them. I'm such an idiot! Authelia's pretty, always has been, but Quentin probably didn't notice until now. And after he eats that Sweetheart Pie, I'll lose him, too. Once she's made him her boyfriend, she won't let him talk to me, not even to say hi in the hallway.

Tears sneak past my eyelids, and sadness sucks me down. I let myself drift away.

"Josephine..."

Shaula.

In the mirror over my vanity, her reflection shimmers as she moves. She's nothing more than a reflection, which helps calm my heartbeat just a little bit. I flick on my bedroom light, hoping she will disappear, but no such luck.

I rub my eyes dry. "Why are you still here? Don't you have voodoo to do?"

Shaula gives me a strange, blank look. "I'm here for you."

Cold creeps over my fingers and toes. I tug my blankets closer. "I'm not a witch."

"Josephine, you have some of the strongest conjure I've felt in ages."

She took those words straight out of Grandma Lula's mouth, years and years ago.

"No," I say. "Every time I try to bake something, cook anything at all, it's a complete disaster. Smoke, fire, you name it. Maybe you weren't watching me then, but I just about burned down Carl and Earl's the other day."

Shaula steps closer within my mirror, until I can see only her lovely face. "Too much of a good thing can be very bad."

I glare at her to hide my fear. "Enough riddles."

Her hair twists against the mirror's edges like caged snakes trying to get out. "Let me make this very plain. You have so much raw power it overflows from you, and not enough control to fashion it into conjure."

I laugh hollowly. "So I'm not trying hard enough?"

"You're trying too hard. You're hungering for too much."

"I don't see anything unusual about what I want." My face heats, because I'm beginning to suspect even I don't know all my wants quite yet.

"Josephine." Shaula smiles a strange, thin smile. "You are far from a usual girl."

"I don't get why you're trying to help me, if that's even what it is."

The stars on her skin dim. "He will come for you like he came for me."

"Who?"

"The Ravenous One."

An invisible fist squeezes my ribs, stealing my breath.

"That name doesn't ring a bell." I shake my head hard. "Can I sleep now? I'd like my normal dreams back, thank you."

"Josephine," she murmurs, "who said this was a dream?"

Sweet Jesus, she's going to crawl out of the mirror. I hurl a hairbrush at the glass. It shatters into glittering shards, and in the sound of breaking, I hear Shaula laughing. My hands clenched, I tiptoe over to the floor.

In each of the shattered pieces, I see only myself reflected.

"*Mon dieu!*" Daddy shouts, his voice muffled.

"Josephine?" Mama calls.

Lord have mercy.

***

Turns out Mama and Daddy think I'm more of a klutz than I imagined. They ate up my story about how I was trying to move my mirror so I could hang a new movie poster, only it slipped out of my sweaty hands and smashed on the floor. Daddy sneaks back to bed, his eyes red-rimmed, leaving us to pick up the pieces.

Mama sighs. "Seven years of bad luck."

I'm not sure I believe it's bad luck, because if I did, it

means a piece of my soul slipped away when the mirror broke. I'm none too happy when I cut myself on the broken glass, and my blood stains where Shaula looked at me.

I could tell Mama. I should tell Mama. But what do I say?

Mama, do you ever wake up with a dictionary in your bed and your handwriting in it?

Ever been stalked by a voodoo spirit, or made the acquaintance of Shaula?

Ever fought a fire-creature trying to burn you alive?

She's going to think I'm plumb crazy. And I'm beginning to think I am.

I wait until all the broken glass is swept up, and follow Mama outside to the garbage can. It's a muggy night, and even the bugs seem sluggish. I still can't keep myself from shivering, for some reason, even when I hug myself.

"Mama?" I say. "Do you know who the Ravenous One is?"

She sighs. "Has everything I ever taught you about conjure fallen clean out of your head?"

Well, probably. "I don't remember you telling me."

She faces me, one hand on her hip. "He's Papa Nom, of course."

"Papa Nom?" It comes out far too loud.

Mama shushes me. "Josephine! The neighbors will hear you."

I peer through the night, trying to spy the clay statue of Papa Nom in our backyard. I see nothing more than a fat, man-shaped blob.

"But why is he the Ravenous One?" I whisper.

Shadows move over Mama's face. "We don't speak of him as such, out of respect, and most witches don't know him by any other name. Seems like nowadays, nobody even remembers who he actually is, besides the spirit who blesses our conjure."

I frown. "The spirit of delicious?"

Mama laughs. "No, honey. Of hunger itself."

Hunger. You're trying too hard. You're hungering for too much.

"No hunger," Mama says, "and nobody would want to eat anything, or even live. Our conjure would be useless, in fact. But there is such a thing as too much hunger, as starvation and famine. That's the job of the Ravenous One."

I swallow hard. "What does he look like?"

Mama locks gazes with me. "A terrible beast with a taste for souls."

My mouth goes bone dry, and the questions on my tongue shrivel up. The black tangle in my dictionary. Devourer. The fire-creature, reaching for me with tentacles. It spoke to me, in a hiss of heat and desire: *I want you.* It knew my name.

He will come for you like he came for me.

Shaula wasn't lying. I'm being hunted, for my very soul.

FOUR

"Shaula?" I whisper. "I believe you now." I stand by my bedroom window and look into the velvety night. Outside, katydids rasp *zit-zit-zit-zit* in a throbbing chorus. "I need your help."

By my vague reflection in the window, the glass ripples like water. For a second I see Shaula standing beside me, but then she's gone.

"Shaula!"

"I have stayed here too long..." she whispers, and I can barely hear her over the katydids.

"You're going to tell me I'm doomed and then leave?" I grip the edge of the windowsill, no matter that splinters are digging into my hands. "You can't do that. You said you were my only hope of help. Are you a liar?"

She speaks so softly I have to hold my breath to listen. "Your... grimoire..."

"Grimoire?" My reflection looks like a madwoman with wild hair and huge, dark eyes. "You're talking nonsense. I don't have any grimoire."

But she is gone.

I climb into bed. Sleep is a long time coming, and entirely empty of dreams.

***

I wake in the gray light of dawn. Groggy, I roll over, and feel something crusty smear my cheek. I lean back and blink until I can see.

Blood.

It puddles on my pillow and streaks my sheets. My heart thuds hollowly in my chest. My face feels hot, then cold, and I have to lie down again. Pain throbs in two pricks on my neck. When I touch my skin, I feel teethmarks.

I was bitten in the night. By who? The Ravenous One?

Why didn't he kill me?

I blow out my breath and clench fistfuls of sheets, dragging myself upright. When I look at it again, there really isn't too much blood gone. Just about as much as if I had a nosebleed and smeared it around in my sleep.

That's what I'll have to tell Mama, until I can figure this out myself.

I dart into the bathroom and lock the door behind me.

My hands shake as I wash myself, pink water swirling down the drain. After a scarf over my scabs, I look as good as new, though I feel more than a bit woozy.

It's barely six o'clock, but Mama is already in the kitchen. This time, she's slicing strawberries superfine for the Sweetheart Pie. My very own mother is creating the thing that will doom me to be friendless forever.

I have two days left before she starts baking.

"Hungry?" Mama says.

I shake my head and lean against the fridge. Not hungry for breakfast, anyway.

Pie or no pie, Authelia has Quentin in her sights. She's going to giggle and play with her hair until he turns into one of those dumb moon-eyed boys.

After that, it will be like Quentin never knew me.

"Sure you're not hungry?" Mama glances up from her strawberries. "You look pale."

"I'm fine, Mama," I say, thinking of her healing conjure. "Just a little tired."

And a little drained of blood, but of course I'm not going to say that.

"Well." Mama wipes red juice from her knife. "If you're too under the weather to help Daddy, come help me today. I'm making deliveries. Doughnuts."

I twist my mouth. "I have a stomachache. I don't want to get carsick."

"Probably from eating too many of those super-special

onion rings."

Daddy comes running downstairs, as if on cue. "What was that about my onion rings?" He flings open the fridge and pulls out a carton of eggs.

"Nothing, Laurent," Mama says. "And don't use all those eggs on breakfast."

"I know." Daddy cracks two eggs over the skillet. "You coming, Jo?"

I chew the inside of my cheek. Mama thinks I ate too many super-special onion rings, but the truth is, I haven't tasted a single one. If I go with Daddy, I can taste plenty of onion rings, for a limited time only. And if I stay—

"Josephine's sick," Mama says. "She's helping me today."

I grimace. "No, thanks. I'd probably be more of a hindrance than a help."

Mama sighs. "Even if you don't have an appetite, eat your breakfast."

"*Bien sûr*," Daddy says.

I manage to escape the kitchen after eating two boiled eggs, a slice of toast, and a glass of orange juice—thankfully without Mama's healing conjure. But all my breakfast starts churning around in my stomach when I see the blood on my pillow again. I flip the pillow over and lie down. My breath escapes me in a whoosh.

Lord, is this how I'm going to spend my summer?

As I bike into Paris, my legs feel heavy. Maybe Shaula will be in the swamp again. My hands clammy, I take the shortcut through the cypresses. Duckweed floats so still and flat on the water that it might as well be a green tile floor.

"Shaula?" I whisper, and feel stupid for doing so. "Shaula!"

Nothing, not even a ripple. A mosquito whines in my ear, then invites three more of her friends. They hover around the bite on my neck, no doubt hungering for my blood. I wince at the thought of a giant mosquito sucking me dry last night.

I really am going to be sick if I keep thinking like this.

I blow out my breath and pedal harder. Today promises to be another scorcher, and sweat already trickles down my back and sticks escapee curls to my forehead, no matter how many times I tame my frizzy hair into a ponytail.

Well, at least the Nebula Theater has air conditioning.

I really do still want to see *Marooned in the Universe*, Quentin or no Quentin. I'm sure Authelia ruined the movie for him, giggling at the intergalactic romance, gasping at the space battles, leaning up close against—

No. Yuck. Let's not imagine that.

The Nebula Theater looks flat and washed-out in the

noon sunlight, all its nighttime glitter and glamour gone. I park my bike and kneel on the sidewalk, fiddling with my rusty old bike lock, which is being stubborn again. By the time I'm done, I'm absolutely parched. I eyeball the Rexall's drugstore, then cave in to temptation.

The moment my shoes hit the black-and-white tiles, I stare at the gleaming chrome of the soda fountain. My mouth starts watering at the promise of my favorite concoction, the black cow, which is root beer and chocolate ice cream. I smile at Will, the cuter of the Rexall's two soda jerks. Then a lady at the counter moves out of my eyesight, and I see a boy sitting on one of the stools. A boy with all-too-familiar pale hair.

"Hell's bells," I mutter.

I try to backpedal out of the drugstore, but it's too late.

"Hey, Josephine!"

My throat feels tight. "Hey, Quentin." It comes out raspy.

A sunny smile brightens his face. "Come sit with me." He pats the stool to his left.

I glare at him. "You're alone?" I half-expect Authelia to waltz out of the ladies' room.

He blinks. "Sorry?"

"Never mind," I say. "Anyway, I'd better hurry before I miss the next showing. Bye." My hand closes on the Rexall's door.

Quentin slurps the last of his soda and darts after me.

"What're you watching?"

I sigh and squint at the baking sun. "*Marooned in the Universe.*"

"Oh!" he says cheerfully. "That was a great movie. I loved the part—"

"Don't," I say. "Just stop spoiling everything. You already ruined my soda."

"But you didn't order a soda."

"Exactly." I push through the Nebula's revolving doors.

Finally, he seems to notice something's wrong. "Are you okay?"

I heave a heavy sigh. "Quentin, are you stupid?" I know I'm being nasty, but I can't stop. "Please don't say yes."

Quentin blinks, his eyes big. "I'm not stupid."

I rake my fingers through my hair. "Then stop acting dumb."

"I'm not!"

I narrow my eyes at him. "You have to dumber than dirt to kiss Authelia McArthur."

"What?" Quentin grabs his head in his hands. "You must be sick, you're talking nonsense. You know I've never kissed a girl in my life." His face turns lobster red when he realizes what he just said.

"Don't you lie to me. I know you did." My eyes are stinging now, so I decide fake-butter popcorn is infinitely more interesting than him.

He steps in front of me, his eyes like blue fire. "I don't

know who told you—"

"Authelia."

"And you believe her?"

I pick up some Tootsie Rolls and pretend to read the label. "You took her to the movies."

"Is that all?" He laughs. "Josephine, we go to the movies all the time."

My throat closes up, and suddenly I'm so mad I can't see straight. I toss the candy back onto the display. "You know what? I have to pee. Don't wait up." I march toward the restrooms, hoping he will take a hint.

Quentin's hot on my tail. "Josephine, please."

"You better not follow me into the *ladies'* room," I say.

He takes me by the hand, gently, and tugs me to a stop. "I know you and Authelia had a big argument, but—"

"A big argument?" I laugh. "You weren't there, were you?"

He shakes his head. "No, but—"

"It was her thirteenth birthday party, Quentin. There were a few billion people there, and every single one of them saw her laugh in my face when she opened my present." I suck in my breath. "It wasn't supposed to be funny."

Quentin rubs the back of his neck. "What did you give her, again?"

My face blazes. "Movie memorabilia."

"Oh?" His eyebrows go up. "What?"

"A collectable doll of Amandine LeClair." Now my face has reached volcanic temperatures. "She said only a baby would want a toy."

"Oh." Quentin clears his throat, not looking at me. "I think I get it."

I laugh. "I don't think you do."

"Don't take it out on me, okay? I can't go around hating everybody you hate."

I swallow back the bitterness and ask the question I've been dreading. "So you like her?"

"Josephine," he says, laughing softly. "You're making mountains out of molehills."

I glare at him, ignoring the little grasshopper-jump of hope inside me. "Am I?"

"We're friends, right? Authelia can't change that."

Oh, but I know her. She's never going to let you talk to me again.

Quentin scrunches his eyebrows, trying hard to smile, but try as I might, I can't smile back. An unnamable feeling swells up inside me, choking my throat, and I blink rapid-fire. I'm not the kind of girl who bursts into tears; but then again, I wasn't the kind of girl who looks at a boy and sees everything she could have had.

"Josephine?" he says.

"I'll see you later," I say, my voice crisp and cold.

"Right."

With that, I flee into the dingy restroom. I see my

reflection in the dull mirror above the sink, and I look so sorrowful that I can't help but laugh, though it's dangerously close to a hiccupping sob. I breathe in slow.

"I don't want to be alone," I whisper.

All you need is a good recipe.

Like a recipe for an ordinary pie to replace the magical one that Authelia ordered. No, like a recipe for friendship forever. If Authelia thinks she can steal Quentin away, I have news for her. He doesn't even belong in her dreams. She can't just march in here with her money and pretend to be better than me at everything. Authelia isn't even a witch—conjure belongs to me. Why shouldn't I take what is rightfully mine?

I might be able to cook up a second chance.

For a good recipe, I'm going to need a good cookbook. I can't use one of Mama's, especially since her Sweetheart Pie takes three days, and I've only got two. I want something quicker, more powerful... maybe I should read Mama's grimoire, where she saves all her most secret recipes. But she'd cook me alive if I so much as touched it.

"Oh," I say softly. "Oh!"

Shaula said I have a grimoire. I think I know what—and where—it is.

***

The sun sinks behind mountains of trash as Sinatra croons

through radio static. I bike through the gates of the town dump and nod at the caretaker, a skinny fellow named Horton, who's watering his weeds in a garden of junked lawn ornaments.

"Josephine!" Horton squints at me like I'm a mirage. "Here to deliver some curly fries?"

I laugh a little. He's a regular at Carl and Earl's, and likes to chat with me and Daddy.

"Afraid not," I say. "I threw something out by accident."

"Oh." He scratches the stubble that creeps from his chin to neck. "Want help looking?"

I shake my head. "No, thanks. Can I borrow a shovel?"

"Sure thing."

Properly armed, I hike to this week's trash. Mixed in with all the newspapers and dirty diapers and food scraps, there's an awful lot of pie, cake, and cookies here—crumbled, smashed, ruined. My heart sinks to my toes. There's a signature pink box of Mama's DeLune DeLuxe Doughnuts, and not a single one eaten.

Now this is peculiar. The people of Paris have always had a taste for Mama's conjure.

I start digging. All the squished dough and rotting fruit and moldy crusts mixes together into a nasty mush of destroyed desserts. What a waste. I get past all the desserts and start going through ordinary trash, which stinks worse, but is less sad to see.

Finally, after more filth than I ever wanted to unearth, there it is.

My dictionary, sparkling clean. I can't believe nothing nasty soaked into it. I scoop the book onto my shovel, just in case, and set it on top of a rusted old bed frame. Fingers not the steadiest in the world, I flip it open and then jump back, as if it might go off like a bomb. The words on those two pages have smudged, their ink wet. A breeze ruffles through more pages, all the words unreadable except for Delicious, along with *Win Quentin*. Cold sweeps over my skin, leaving goosebumps in its wake.

Ruined words slither across the pages like leeches, then curl into a sentence: *I found you.*

A whirlwind of ash and shredded trash whistles past. As it dies away, I hear laughter. Not Horton, laughing at some dumb joke on the radio, but a nasty sort of chuckle rustier than that old bed frame. A maybe-not-human sort of chuckle.

My heartbeat kicks into a higher gear. I slam the dictionary shut and sprint down the trash hill, trying not to tumble and skid down through broken glass and spiky scraps of metal. The dictionary feels weirdly hot in my hands, but that could just be because I'm sweating so much. What happens when people throw away conjure? Does the magic warp and twist and go so bad that it wants revenge?

Out of the corner of my eye, a small and white

something moves.

I freeze, because against all better judgment, I want to at least see what I'm running from. It's a little porcelain baby angel with closed eyes and broken wings. Only, its hands aren't stuck in perpetual prayer. It's climbing out of the rubble.

I watch the angel scuttle closer, surprisingly fast, while this tight feeling builds and builds in my legs. I want to run, I should run, why am I just standing here watching this cursed figurine come close enough to touch me?

The angel's eyes spring open. They are as red as the fires of hell.

I swallow a scream and grab the nearest blunt object—in this case, a metal pipe. I whack the angel, shattering its face, and it stops moving.

"Sweet Jesus, I've had enough of this," I say.

I stare at the empty space behind the angel's broken face. A screeching noise scrapes my ears. Old bedsprings start uncoiling into rusty tentacles, slithering toward my ankles like they mean to drag me down. This time, I do scream. And then I do this amazing hurdle good enough for the Olympics and practically fly out of there.

As I sprint down the slope, the dictionary grows hotter in my hands—no, my grimoire. A bedspring whips forward and slices my leg like a sharp tongue tasting blood. I grit my teeth and leap onto the dirt path, away from any garbage. There's a terrible groan, like metal at its breaking point. I look back and see the bedsprings recoiling. They burrow down into the trash, and then everything is still and silent.

Ahead, Horton stands with his back to me, as if contemplating the sunset.

"Horton!" I cry. "Did you just see that?"

He makes a sort of neutral, "Mmm," sound.

"Horton?"

He faces me, and murky white clouds his eyes. His smile looks more like a rabid dog baring its teeth. When he speaks, it isn't with Horton's voice, and I don't know if I'll ever hear it again. "You belong to me."

It's the desire-filled hiss of the fire-creature, of the Ravenous One.

FIVE

I'm looking into the eyes of Hunger himself. I don't know what to say, except, "Why?"

The Ravenous One is silent for a moment, save for the rasping of his breath. Maybe nobody has ever asked him that before. "I haven't tasted a soul like yours in years. Delicious. I will relish every drop of your blood."

My fingers dart to the teethmarks on my neck. He bit me already? Why not kill me then?

"No thanks," I say, glad I sound more flippant than terrified, which I truly am.

His lips pull back to bare all his teeth, and he licks the air like he's tasting my scent.

"Get out of my way," I say, and the fear shows in my voice this time.

The Ravenous One laughs. Drool drips down his chin like a dog slobbering.

In my hands, the grimoire grows too hot to touch. I fling it open and see the words, bold and big, stretched across two pages: *Let me go.*

I drop the grimoire, and it thuds on the dirt. The ink of the words bursts into a black cloud, like a puffball mushroom. It smells like a graveyard rotting in the summer heat. I breathe in a mouthful, cough, and all my limbs stiffen. Blackness spreads through my veins and sinks into my bones. In my mouth, I taste death.

Words leave my lips. "It's been a long time, hasn't it?"

I don't sound like myself anymore, my voice lower, sweeter. When I try to move, I can't. I'm a puppet. Possessed.

The Ravenous One's face twists. "You?"

My hands move out to my sides, away from my body, as if I'm daring him to stick a dagger in my heart. My skin looks pure black, glittering with stars that catch the fire of the dying sun. A white gown floats like a ghost over my clothes.

I'm the night-skinned lady. Is Shaula possessing me, or am I possessing her?

"I'm already dead," I say—she says. "You can't kill me."

The Ravenous One's nostrils flare. A moaning growl rises from his throat.

I pick up the grimoire. My back straight, my heartbeat as steady as a metronome, I stroll straight past the Ravenous One. I abandon my bike in the dirt, pass through the gates of the town dump, and don't spare a backward glance.

There's a deep rumbling. This time, I do look.

Horton is gone. Broken glass and metal shards fountain from the dump and arch over the chain-link fence, ready to rain down on my head.

My mouth opens. "Run."

The possession leaves me in a rush, and my legs feel like noodles. I stare at the hail of garbage for half a second, then bolt down the road at a dead sprint. Glass shatters and metal rattles on the fence behind me. I run until my muscles burn and my breath turns ragged. The grimoire gets heavier and heavier in my hands.

I glance back, and the dump is far behind. I'm alone.

I stop, gasping, and drop the grimoire on the side of the road. It falls open to a mess of ruined words. Doubled over, I cough so hard I retch, then spit out some black dust onto the pages of the grimoire. It vanishes into the paper.

The ruined words squirm into new shapes. *Go home.*

I do as I'm told.

Of course I don't have my bike, so I have to walk the whole way back. The air feels thick in my throat, like waterlogged cotton, and I want to scream at all the chirping, trilling, rasping bugs to shut up for awhile.

I keep glancing at my hands, which aren't night-skinned anymore. Shaula possessed me and made me look like her long enough to fool the Ravenous One. That much

I'm sure of. As for the rest, I'm going to have to ask her.

Judging by the height of the moon, it must be at least ten o'clock when I get home. My feet ache. I'm still holding my grimoire, but I'm not sure I want Mama asking questions about it. She's going to swoop down on me the minute I set foot inside, judging by the light coming from the kitchen window. I hide the heavy book beneath the porch steps and pray some possum doesn't eat it after everything I went through.

Sure enough, Mama ambushes me by the door. "Josephine Elle DeLune!"

I realize I must look a frightful mess. "Crashed my bike," I say. "Had to walk partway home." Which isn't a complete lie.

She grabs me by my shoulders and turns me around to inspect me. "Are you hurt?"

I hesitate, then shake my head. Beside being possessed and nearly killed, I'm okay. Those bedsprings slashed my leg, but they're shallow cuts.

Mama's jaw tightens. "Supper is ice cold. You're just going to have to choke it down."

I doubt that's true, since it's another muggy night, but I don't feel like arguing. I let her serve me a plate of lukewarm fried perch and collard greens cooked within an inch of their lives, like any good vegetables. Not a drop of conjure, though. An invisible fist tightens around my stomach. That's pretty strange.

Mama sits opposite me, cradling a mug of coffee dregs. She stares at a newspaper with bloodshot eyes. "Did you see this?"

"See what?" I eat another forkful of collard greens.

Mama shushes me. "Don't wake your daddy. He's had a long day."

I lower my voice. "We get the Paris Gazette now?"

"No, it was wrapped around a trout I bought."

"Well, what's so interesting about it?"

Mama smoothes the newspaper flat. It's quite crumpled around the edges, like someone clenched it with sweaty fingers. "'Beware of Baked Black Magic. Authorities grow increasingly concerned about dangerously high levels of black magic in Monroe County, Missouri. What is the source of this unholy, unhealthy witchcraft? Homemade baked goods are suspected, and residents are urged to buy only from trusted sources, such as breads, cakes, cookies, and other products available from reputable neighborhood supermarkets. Experts in the medical community seek to debunk the common misconception that small quantities of enchanted foodstuffs are harmless, as recent evidence proves otherwise. The consequences of eating baked goods tainted with black magic may range from food poisoning to, in rare cases, death. Housewives are encouraged to shop wisely.'"

My mouth hangs open, my half-chewed collard greens on display, so I swallow. I don't have the heart to tell her about all the desserts in the dump.

Mama breathes out through her nose in a hiss. "Came out on Sunday."

"Who wrote it?" I say.

She squints at the newspaper. "Mr. Riley E. Bates. Don't know him."

"That article is a load of horse manure, pardon my French." I wrinkle my nose. "And even if people don't like the sound of black magic, why would anybody in Paris think that you would poison your loyal customers?"

"Would you drink milk if the newspaper said there might be arsenic in it?"

I don't know what to say to that.

I finish my supper in silence, and Mama keeps sitting at the table, her eyes looking at something faraway. After I put my plate in the sink, I hug her shoulders, and she squeezes my hand. My throat tightens up. I hate seeing her look so tired and defeated. She knows as well as I do we'd be twice as poor without her customers.

"Well," she sighs, "at least we have the Sweetheart Pie. Unless that order gets canceled."

I don't tell her that's what I was hoping.

***

Midnight rolls around before Mama finally goes to bed. The moment her light is out, I grab my shoes and tiptoe downstairs. I'm not the slightest bit sleepy, and I have business to attend to. Shaula might not have thought my bike was all that important, but that doesn't mean I have to let it rust to bits in the dump.

It's a clear night, and all the stars are out. The sky ripples above like somebody threw a stone in a pond. I walk beneath the ripples and crane my neck upward. A glowing outline takes shape among the constellations—the figure of a woman. Shaula. Her sleek black skin glistens with stars so beautiful my eyes tear up. She drifts down from the sky and touches the ground as lightly as a dandelion seed.

"Shaula!" I whisper.

She touches her finger to her lips, then beckons for me to follow her. I walk with her into the backyard, near the statue of Papa Nom.

"I thought you said you couldn't stay," I say.

She smiles. "I borrowed some of your power."

"My... power?"

She cups my face in her hands. I flinch, startled. This is the first time she's touched me, and her skin feels as cool and vague as mist.

She slides her fingers down the bite on my neck. "Only a little blood was needed."

My stomach clenches, and I back away from her. "You bit me? Not the Ravenous One?"

"Yes, *ma chère*." She laughs, not unkindly. "You have

72

my blood in you, enough to strengthen my ties to the mortal world."

Her blood, in me. I'm not sure I want to know what she means.

"You look confused," Shaula says. "Did no one tell you?"

"Tell me what?"

"Who I truly am. Shaula D'Arcantel."

That's not ringing any bells. "Oh?"

"Have you not studied your family tree? I'm the mother of Celestine Leroy, the grandmother of Alula Bellerose, the great-grandmother of Clara DeLune, and the great-great-grandmother—" she takes a breath "—of you."

I'm clean out of words for a minute or two. "But you fought my great-great-grandma."

"Josephine, I'm afraid that's a lie. I was there, I know what truly happened."

I rub my forehead with my knuckles. "What did happen?"

Shaula stares into the darkness, a faraway look on her face. "It was 1879, the year my daughter Celestine turned eleven. Gabriel de Witte—her father—left me for his first wife, and I had little more to my name than a bad reputation."

"Why?"

"I was very like you, Josephine." She meets my gaze. "I wanted so many things I shouldn't have. The lure of dark conjure tempted me like it never had before. My power was raw, my hunger too great."

There is a such thing as dark conjure, which is sort of like the difference between angel food cake and devil's food cake. One of them is lighter, airier, and not as strong; the other is rich, heavy, and apt to summon real devils. I don't know much about the summoning process, just that you generally don't want to.

"One night in the swamps of Louisiana," Shaula says, "the Ravenous One came for me."

A shiver passes over my skin. I know what must have happened next.

"I fought him," she says, "but I was not strong enough."

"Did he devour your soul?" I say.

"No. I took it myself." Her eyes gleam with a curious mix of triumph and sadness. "I knew that if he consumed me, he would gain my memories, my talents, and only grow even more powerful. You see, the Ravenous One was once no more than Hunger, a nameless force, but after his first taste of a witch's soul..."

"You mean to say that he has all the conjure of all the witches he's ever eaten?"

"Yes," she says. "He has particular tastes, and devours only the most powerful."

I feel cold and small. I hug myself tight, but it doesn't help in the slightest.

Shaula strokes my hair. Her fingers slip through my

curls like a ghost's. "After I died, I became as you see me now. I could only watch as my daughter, Celestine, passed through her life without me. Gabriel raised her, and he turned her against conjure and spoke only ill of me. It's no wonder you have heard only lies."

"I knew Celestine," I say. "She got real old. Eighty-something, I think. I remember being scared of her when I was a little girl. She was always going on about superstitions, and talked about conjure like it was something shameful."

"I know," she says. "I saw you meet. And I saw her die."

My throat tightens. "I'm sorry."

"No need to be sorry. I have been fortunate to see my family untouched by the Ravenous One... at least, until you were born. Did you know I came into this world in 1843, one hundred years before you? It's fascinating to consider."

Her voice sounds deadly soft. I fight a shiver.

"Alula was right," she says. "You will be one of the strongest witches among us. Together, we will find a way to save you."

"Thank you," I say.

Shaula smiles. "I have faith in you."

Try as I might, I can't smile back. Maybe I could if I had faith in myself.

We walk back to the dump. Pelting rain slicks my coat and makes me shiver. Half the raindrops trickle down Shaula's skin, while the rest ripple straight through her. A wormy smell of dirt, fallen leaves, and rotting things soaks the air.

I glance at Shaula. "Who says the Ravenous One isn't still here?"

She puts her cold hand on my shoulder. "It takes too much power to manifest again so soon, even for him. He is waiting."

"That makes me feel a whole lot better," I mutter.

I had the good sense to bring a flashlight with me, but not enough sense to check the batteries. The light keeps flickering, no matter how much I whack it against my leg, and barely does anything in this inky darkness. I swing the light around and keep my eyes peeled for my bike, but I'm spotting nothing but trash. Static crackles from Horton's radio. Nobody ever turned it off. I shudder, and Shaula's fingers tighten on my shoulder.

"I want to show you something," she says.

I swallow hard and nod.

She leads me away from the path and up a hill of garbage. We're awfully close to where the Ravenous One attacked me this afternoon. My legs are wobbling like Jell-O, but I force myself to keep walking. I want to see this.

"Shine your light over there." Shaula points one finger

into the darkness.

I whack my flashlight again, then raise it in that direction.

A man stands at the top of the hill, his back to us, his clothes drenched with rain. He crouches, grabbing something from the trash and shoving it into his mouth like a clumsy baby. Bits fall to the ground as he chews.

"Horton?" My voice is squeezed by my tight throat.

"Look at him," Shaula says.

My flashlight flickers, then steadies. The man straightens with a low moan, like he's hurt. He shuffles away from us.

"Horton!"

The man stops, then turns. It is Horton. His face is as white as flour, streaked with dark by his mouth. He sways on his feet, and moans. Now that he's closer, I can see it more clearly. Horton's eyes look like zeros. Empty.

"Good lord." I clutch my flashlight like a baseball bat. "Shaula, he's a zombie."

"Yes," she says, matter-of-factly.

Horton's throat moves like he's going to vomit. A strangled word comes out. "Hungry."

"Hungry?"

Horton lifts his arms to me. "Cake."

"Cake?"

"Cake."

I back up and glance at my feet. There's a moldy angel

food cake. Grimacing, I dig out a fistful and hurl it at the zombie. Horton bends stiffly, then falls flat on his face. He crawls to the cake and eats it like a dog.

A crazy laugh bubbles up inside me. A cake-eating zombie.

Horton staggers to his feet, his mouth streaked with frosting. "Cake," he says, and he sounds almost satisfied.

I nod. "You like it?"

He moans low in his throat and shuffles nearer, his stiff arms reaching for me. I back away from him, looking for more cake. I grab a doughnut and straighten so I can throw it to him. He's almost close enough to touch me.

"Why does he want cake," I ask Shaula, "and not brains and guts?"

"Because the Ravenous One does not hunger for flesh," she says. "He can taste your mother's conjure baked into that cake."

My throat clenches. "He's still possessing Horton?"

"No." Shaula's eyes are as black as the sky. "This zombie—Horton—has been cursed with the hunger of the Ravenous One. He will crave conjure until it devours him from the inside out, until it becomes too late to save him."

"We can save him?" I say. "But he's... dead. Undead."

"There is a countercurse," Shaula says.

I swallow hard. "Tell me what it is."

"I will take care of him." There isn't a trace of uncertainty or worry in her voice. She stands between me and the zombie, and points down the hill of trash. "Your bicycle is waiting for you there. Take it, and go home."

"Shaula," I whisper. "You're not going to kill him, are you?"

"No," she says. "I will take care of him."

"But..."

She doesn't touch me, or give me a smile, but I see a hint of sadness sharpen her eyes. "This is what must be done. Go."

And so I leave her and Horton behind, and bike the long way home alone.

SIX

One day until Mama bakes her strawberry-rhubarb Sweetheart Pie.

The thought sneaks back into my head while I'm lying in bed that morning, and I feel rotten as soon as I think such a selfish thing. Shaula hasn't shown up since last night, and I have nobody to talk to about Horton. I don't have a clue if he had family—he kept to himself, and I only ever saw him either at the dump or Carl and Earl's.

All I know is that it's my fault Horton is a zombie now.

I need to stop the Ravenous One, and I need to learn how.

I grab my grimoire out from under my bed and sit with it open between my knees. As soon as the pages fall flat, the words begin slithering again. I lift my fingers from the book, afraid to touch the ink, and wait for them to settle.

All you need is a good recipe.

"I already know that," I say.

The words reshape themselves. *You know what you want, Josephine. You should not wait. Learn how to control this hunger through conjure, and then you will control Hunger himself.* My face gets hot. Shaula is definitely back in my grimoire. And she has definitely been snooping on my secret desires again.

"So I'm supposed to bake some conjure for Quentin? Before Mama does?"

Yes.

And then the words in the grimoire drift apart into gibberish again.

As soon as Daddy is at work, and Mama is away visiting a coven of witches one county over, I do something drastic.

It's late in the afternoon, and clumsy June bugs keep crashing against the screen door. Sweat drips down my forehead and the glass pitcher on the table. Cleon's off charming some girl or another, so I have the house to myself.

And the kitchen.

I tiptoe over to the tall bookshelf by the kitchen door, even though nobody's here to see me, and tilt my head sideways. *The Joy of Cooking, 1001 Easy Kitchen Spells, The New American Conjure Cookbook...* Mama calls these her second-rate recipes, since no witch worth her salt would write down anything really good outside of her grimoire, but unless I want to steal her secrets, this is all I've got. I slide out the *Conjure Cookbook* and prop it open on the edge of the shelf. The pages crinkle in my shaking hands.

Yes, these are some of Mama's recipes, all right.

PERFECT PICKLE LOAF

Useful for curing lovesickness of every kind, the Perfect Pickle Loaf is also a tidy way to fashion pork leftovers into a daintier confection. Green olives are a must, as they will add immensely to the handsomeness and flavor of this dish.

I wrinkle my nose. "Pickle loaf" is a nicer way of saying, "head cheese," which is a nicer way of saying, "boiling a pig's head and then mixing all the meaty bits with gelatin." That's not going to help me win over Quentin. I put back the cookbook, then, by accident, knock over some books on a lower shelf. They avalanche onto my toes.

"Jiminy cricket!" I bite the inside of my cheek. "Lord, that hurts."

I kick the bookshelf in revenge, and almost stomp on a leather-bound book splayed on the linoleum. I pick it up and dust it off. No title on the spine, or the cover. Is this a cookbook? Cursive covers the yellowed pages, the words tiny and cramped, without very much in the way of spaces in between. It looks awfully familiar.

I try reading some of the recipe names out loud. "'Charlotte's Own Sweet Rice. With just a sprinkling of raisins and fortune, perfect for any occasion.' 'Greatness Gravy. Will make anything else taste great.'" I flip farther through the book. "'Persnickety Pastries. For the pickiest of eaters, or folks with peckish appetites.'"

Oh, this must be Grandma Lula's! Peckish appetites are her greatest enemy.

There's no rhyme or reason to the recipes, which look like they've been concocted by generations of witches. I see a few familiar dishes, but not much that Mama usually cooks. I keep my eyes peeled for the word "friendship."

Aha!

FORGET-ME-NOT PIE

A cherry pie to make any friendship unforgettable. A practical solution for faraway or fair-weather friends. Be careful when measuring for this recipe, as it can be overpowering in a jiffy. Tastes especially nice served with vanilla ice cream.

It's not a strawberry-rhubarb pie, so I can't fool Mama, but Quentin won't even know. I can swap the pies right before delivery.

Forget-Me-Not Pie has pretty standard ingredients, with cherries and flour and such, but that's not counting 1 stick full moon butter, ½ tablespoon dried wormwood leaves, a dash of rosewater, and a drop of baker's blood. And where on earth am I going to find 3 fresh peahen eggs? The supermarket doesn't sell *that*.

I blow out my breath. "Cherries. We have to have cherries."

Mama just baked some cherry tarts… and there are a handful of cherries left. Enough for only a small pie, but that should work.

"Wormwood leaves?" I sound a bit more hopeful.

I rummage through the cabinets and find a tiny bottle of dusty green wormwood leaves. There's no sign of rosewater, and Mama hasn't churned any full moon butter since last month. Besides, I can't get started without the peahen eggs.

I stare at my reflection in the kitchen window. "This pie is impossible."

"The only thing impossible is your attitude, *ma chère*."

I jump back, almost knocking the wormwood onto the floor.

Shaula steps beside my reflection in the window. She looks faint, her outline wavering in the sun and shadows. "You know where to find the ingredients you need."

"I do?"

"For the butter," Shaula's fading voice is hard to hear, "try Aloysius."

"The ice cream truck man?"

"You may know him as such."

"Wait," I say. "Where are you going?"

"Josephine." She's almost gone, her voice a whisper. "Good luck."

A breeze sways a shadow across her face, and Shaula disappears.

"Well," I say, "here goes nothing."

I hop on my bike and start pedaling toward Paris.

It's a blue-sky day, so Aloysius must be out selling ice cream. Soon enough, I hear "Pop Goes the Weasel" tinkling down the tree-lined street.

Aloysius tips his white hat to me and stops his truck. "Hungry for some ice cream?"

I climb off my bike and walk it closer. "Sure," I say slowly.

I inspect his bright smile and the sweat shining on his brow. He looks like a completely normal ice cream truck man. I pat my purse, double-checking that those five whole dollars from my allowance still exist.

"What do you want?"

I arch my eyebrows. "What do you have?"

He laughs. "All kinds of flavors. Chocolate, vanilla, strawberry—"

"I'm looking for something more *unusual*."

"Unusual it is!" Aloysius's smile doesn't falter. "Pistachio, chocolate chip, butter—"

"Butter?"

"Butterscotch? Sure!" He lumbers to his feet and climbs

into the back of the truck.

"How about full moon butter?"

He stops short and looks at me, his eyes popping out a little more than usual. "Now why would a girl like you be asking for that?"

"I need it," I murmur, "for a recipe. If you catch my drift."

Aloysius strokes his mustache and stares at me.

"I have money," I say.

He rummages in the cooler, then returns with a box of butter. I raise my eyebrows at the picture on the box, a lady wearing deerskins.

"Now, this ain't Land O' Lakes." He wiggles his eyebrows. "That's camouflage."

"May I have a taste?"

Aloysius nods and slides a wax-wrapped stick of butter from the box. With a pocket knife, he shaves a curl of butter and passes it to me. I put it on my tongue and let it melt. The silvery flavor of moonlight spreads in my mouth.

I nod. "That's good full moon butter."

"Thanks," Aloysius says. "I get it from a lady up in Shelbina."

"How much for the stick?"

"Four dollars."

"Four dollars!" I'm sure my eyes look even buggier than his. "You're crazy."

Aloysius shakes his head. "Ice cream is only twenty-five cents," he says cheerfully.

I put my hands on my hips. "Now, I don't know what that witch up in Shelbina told you, but full moon butter ain't that special. If I weren't in such a hurry, I'd churn up a batch myself, but it's nearly the new moon, so here we are."

He laughs and turns back into his truck. I hear him mutter, "Spitting image of Alula."

"Alula who?" I say.

He brushes away my question.

I snap my fingers. "You mean Alula Bellerose? Lula? She's my grandmother."

Aloysius gives me this peculiar crossbreed of a smile and a wince, like I've caught him with his hand in the cookie jar. "There's only one Alula Bellerose."

"How did you know Grandma Lula? Are you from Louisiana?"

Aloysius strokes his mustache some more. "In a manner of speaking. I was born in Charleston, Missouri, but I sold ice cream round New Orleans for years. Ice cream and, you know, other things. Alula was a treat to work with."

That must be how Shaula knew about him—she's been keeping tabs on Grandma Lula.

"Grandma Lula sure knows how to cook up conjure," I say.

He smiles bashfully. "She's a real sweet lady."

"Sweet? Well, I suppose that's one way to describe her."

Aloysius laughs. "When I told her I was moving back up to Missouri, she told me to keep an eye out for you and your mama. It's clear she misses you both."

I cock my head. "Just how well do you know my Grandma Lula, anyway?"

He ducks his head and fiddles with the Land O' Lakes box. "Oh, we're friends."

Uh-huh. I strongly suspect Aloysius was courting Grandma Lula, and didn't get very far. She's been a widow for years now, ever since Grandpa Emmett passed away in an unfortunate boating accident on the bayou.

"Maybe you'd consider giving me a preferred customer discount?"

Aloysius folds his arms across his barrel chest. "Try me."

"I'm not paying a cent over three dollars."

"Three fifty."

"Three. And that's final."

"Fair enough."

I cough up my valuable savings, and he hands me the full moon butter.

Aloysius beams at me. "Pleasure doing business with you. Have a nice day!"

I wave goodbye, tuck the butter into my backpack, and climb onto my bike. As I start pedaling, the wind carries the faraway sound of a wailing, "Help! Help!"—nothing but one of those silly peacocks at the McArthur mansion.

Peacocks. Of course!

The McArthurs have a flock of mostly boy peacocks, but I've certainly seen a few brownish peahens. That's where I can get my eggs for the Forget-Me-Not Pie! They won't miss three piddly eggs now, will they?

I swerve toward the peacocks and pedal harder.

Good thing I used to be friends with Authelia. I smile bitterly. I know exactly where to look first. Behind the pool in their backyard, hidden under some glossy magnolia trees, there's a tiny barn where they keep the peacocks after dark. Otherwise some wandering panther might gobble them all up, as Mrs. McArthur loves worrying.

I ditch my bike under a hedge and creep closer to the barn.

Outside, a few peahens scratch around the dust. A big granddaddy of a peacock stands guard near the open door. He tilts back his head and screams, "Help! Help!" then looks sideways at me with his beady little eye.

I stride straight toward the peacock and flap my hands at him. "Shoo."

The peacock's feathers bristle, but he scuttles out of my way. I dart past him and sneak into the cool dusk of the barn. There in the straw, two peahens sit on nests and blink at me. There's also a third nest with no peahen guarding it. I kneel by the nest and find four little brown-speckled eggs. I scoop up three of them.

"Help! Help!" screams the granddaddy peacock, right in my ear.

I juggle the eggs, almost dropping them, and jump to my feet. "Stupid bird! Get!"

The peacock fans his wings and rushes at me, his beak open wide. I sprint out of the barn before he can bite me on the butt, then keep running. The peacock chases me, and I have to leap over a low fence to escape him.

"Good lord!" I gasp.

Panting, I kneel on the ground and gently tuck the eggs into my backpack. I grab my bike and walk it over the lawn. The peacock screams at me again, and I twist around to make sure he's not following me. He's guarding the barn again.

"Nasty bird," I mutter.

"What are you doing here?" says a breathy voice.

I turn my head around so fast I just about give myself whiplash.

Authelia stands in the middle of the lawn with her hands on her hips. She's wearing a glamorous sheer cover-up over a red swimsuit with tiny white polka dots. A swimsuit I would love to have, as much as I hate to admit it.

"Authelia!" My brain whizzes as I think fast. "I was looking for you."

"Me?" She squints. "What for?"

"To apologize," I say.

Authelia's mouth drops. "Oh. Why?"

"For being so rude at Carl and Earl's," I lie, even though she was at least ten times ruder. "That wasn't very nice of me."

She stares at me, her mouth still open, and I keep waiting for a fly to buzz inside.

I try my hardest to look like I am genuinely sorry. "I'd better let you go."

Authelia narrows her eyes. "Wait. You biked all the way here to tell me that?"

"It's not that far." I sling my backpack on. "And we used to be friends."

Her cheeks flush. "Well, not anymore. So don't go trespassing in my backyard." But her words sound feeble, like she's reading lines.

"You could at least accept my apology," I mutter.

And apologize to *me* for being so nasty, though I don't say that.

Authelia twists her mouth like she sucked on a lemon. "Apology accepted."

I climb onto my bike. I'm almost free and clear... only now I feel a teensy bit bad about stealing eggs from her family. She hesitates, then tugs her cover-up closer around her shoulders. I tense up, afraid she's going to ask why I have a backpack.

"You could do better, you know," she says, as bossy as a princess.

"What?" I grip my handlebars, ready to get going.

"If you tried a little harder, you could be more popular."

My throat tightens. "Popular? Who says I want to be popular?"

She squints like I'm speaking gibberish. "So you could actually have friends?"

"Look where that got you," I say.

Authelia frowns, and I start pedaling out of there before she can figure out I insulted her. Wind stings my eyes and whooshes in my ears. The Forget-Me-Not Pie. That's what I need to think about now, not Authelia's stupid words.

All have left is the rosewater. Maybe I know where to find that, too…

I hurry back home and lean my bike against the Osage orange tree. I'm still the only one here. I jog upstairs to my bedroom and fling open the door to my closet. There, lying in a dusty cardboard box, is a miniature bottle of perfume that came with a doll I lost along time ago. I twist open the cheap plastic stopper and sniff. Rosewater.

Back in the kitchen, I lay Grandma Lula's cookbook flat on the counter with a thud.

Ready, set, go.

***

Two hours into my adventure, and I'm hunched over the cookbook, my eyes stinging and dry, my hair a flour-dusted disaster. I know because when I took a bathroom break, I just about scared myself half to death. Smoke drifts in a haze above the kitchen, thanks to me setting my attempt at dough on fire purely by accident. Good thing I hadn't added the peahen eggs yet. Otherwise, I'd be totally ruined.

Conjure ain't easy, as Mama would say.

"Slowly," I whisper to myself. "Carefully."

I tip a cup of sugar over a bowl, my eyes half-closed. I hum under my breath, trying to lull myself into a trance. *Sugar for joy.* That's what Mama always says, and that's what I concentrate on. The sugar pours with a rustling tinkle. I peek at it. Every crystal glows from the inside out, carrying my power into the bowl.

Smoke rises to my nose, carrying the scent of burnt sugar. I tilt the cup upright. Only a few of the crystals look blackened. I scoop them out with a spoon. Next, I grab a bag of flour. I've got to be extra careful, because flour dust can catch fire and set the air itself ablaze. Mama tells stories of witches burning themselves to death. Luckily, flour is a plain ingredient in conjure, without much magic of its own.

I add the flour without disaster, then half a tablespoon of wormwood, then a dash of rosewater. Heady perfumes dizzy me, like I'm breathing by the flowers of a jungle. Three peahen eggs, crack, crack, crack. One stick of full moon butter. I roll up my sleeves and massage the rich gold yolks and butter into the dry ingredients. My fingertips tingle, and a shiver runs down my spine. I clench the dough in my hands, twisting more magic into it, enchanting it with everything I don't know how to say to Quentin.

Too much of a good thing can be very, very bad.

I blink hard. No. Too much conjure, and it's ruined. I lift my hands above my head, sweating, trembling all over. The dough waits, white and shapeless, in its bowl. This is the farthest I've ever got through a recipe. I'm going to do this. I'm going to bake my first pie. All I have to do now is pit the cherries and mix the filling.

The rusty screen door hinges squeal. I jump and slam the cookbook shut.

Cleon strolls into the kitchen, and his eyebrows go heavenward. "What in the name of Betty Crocker are you trying to cook?"

"Nothing you'd want to eat," I say.

He tries to swipe a crumble of dough, and I trap his fingers with Grandma Lula's cookbook. "What's that book?" he says.

"Nothing you'd want to read."

He grabs the end of the cookbook. We tussle in a tug-of-war, and he wins.

"Cleon!" I say. "Don't you dare tell Mama and Daddy."

"About what?" He flips open the cookbook. "Hey, is this Grandma Lula's handwriting?"

"Maybe."

He squints at me. "Are you trying conjure?"

"What do you think?" I shove my hair back from my face and plant my hand on my hip, trying to mimic Mama. "Now Cleon, if you help me out here, I might be able to help you later, if you get the picture."

"Oh?" A smile spreads on his face. "What happens if you burn down the kitchen first?"

Anger coils inside me like a snake. "I'm not, and I'm so close to finishing this recipe. I don't need you barging in here and messing it up, okay?"

"Okay!" He steps away from me. "Sorry, I thought you hated conjure."

I grit my teeth. "Just let me do this. That's all I'm asking."

"Sure thing," Cleon says. "I'm going to give you and your conjure some space."

True to his word, my brother leaves me in peace. I grab a paring knife and start pitting cherries. Dark red juice slicks my fingers and splatters my apron. I lick the sourness away, then turn the paring knife on my finger. I slide the blade along my fingertip and hiss at the pain, then squeeze a drop of blood into the cherries. It vanishes instantly, red on red. My heartbeat thumps in my ears as I stir the blood and fruit together.

Finally, after a pinch of cinnamon, I smooth the top crust over the pie and slide the knife one, two, three times to let steam escape. As a final touch, I cut a heart shape from the top and lay this dough beside the glistening red. When I open the oven, heat washes over me like a dragon breathing out. Dizzy, I clench the edges of the pie dish. I'd rather burn myself than drop it. Squinting, I slide the pie into the oven.

After only thirty minutes or so, the most absolutely amazing aroma wafts from the baking pie and drifts through the whole kitchen—sweetness mixed with a dark, spicy incense. I close my eyes and hug myself tight.

The timer dings. I take the pie out.

Cherry juice spills from the heart shape in the crust, as red as Valentine's Day hearts. My mouth aches so hard it hurts. When I set the pie on a cooling rack, a trickle of blood drips off my finger. I'm still bleeding. I lick it away impatiently.

My masterpiece is complete. Forget-Me-Not Pie.

With the scent of magic still in my hair, I hide the pie in one of Mama's trademark pink boxes, then hide that the back of the freezer. I scrub the kitchen until not a speck of conjure remains, then soak in the bathtub.

A giddy tingling dances in my ribs like fireflies. Is this what it feels like to be powerful?

I fall asleep smiling. Shaula doesn't visit my dreams.

SEVEN

Mama finishes baking her strawberry-rhubarb Sweetheart Pie that very next day. I feel horrible watching her do all that work for nothing, but I feel even worse imagining Quentin falling for Authelia because of it. Romance already ruined Authelia—I don't want her dragging Quentin onto dates. Why would you even go to a movie with somebody if you're going to smooch and slurp through the whole thing?

Maybe my friends have outgrown me.

I grimace and shake that thought away. What Authelia wants to do to Quentin isn't fair. He's my friend, not her *boy*friend.

As soon as Mama leaves the pie out of her sight, I swap it with my Forget-Me-Not Pie.

What do I do with the old one? I stare at the golden crust and sugar sprinkled on top. It's still warm. It looks delicious.

Sometimes you have to make sacrifices. Mama's pie goes into the garbage can.

I run upstairs and put on the cutest sundress I own: pink, printed with little cherries. I smile at how fitting they are. When I run back downstairs, Mama is already pinning on her pillbox hat and grabbing her car keys.

"Where are you going, Mama?" I say, like I don't already know.

"Making deliveries. You want to come?"

"Sure!" I hope that didn't sound too chipper.

Mama purses her lips, but doesn't say anything.

We back from the garage in Mama's brand-spanking new 1955 DeSoto Fireflite convertible in Carnival Red and Surf White. Worth hundreds and hundreds of DeLune DeLuxe doughnuts, cakes, and pastries, baked for years.

"Top down?" Mama says.

I grin. "Top down."

I pull my hair back in a ponytail so the wind won't make it too crazy. We cruise in style through downtown Paris. Mama revs the engine at a four-way stop, then zooms through a left turn. I clutch the Forget-Me-Not Pie box in my lap.

For our first stop, Mama pulls over outside a pretty white house that just happens to belong to the Cole family. I sit up straighter, my heartbeat thumping about a million miles an hour. A skinny lightning-bolt of a greyhound streaks from the backyard, a tennis ball wedged between his teeth, his tongue flapping in the wind. He's a handsome dog, all long bones and lean muscle, with tan fur like a lion's.

"Flash, fetch! Fetch!" Quentin sprints after his dog, his cheeks red, then skids to a stop.

We stare at each other for a second, and I can tell by his smile that he's trying to apologize. Lord, why I am blushing?

"Good morning, ladies," he says to me and Mama.

Mrs. Cole runs up wearing curlers in her hair and a water-splotched apron. "Quentin!" she calls in her canary voice. "Didn't you hear what I said about not playing with that greyhound in the mud? He just got a bath."

"Good morning, Mrs. Cole," Mama says.

"Oh!" Mrs. Cole blinks and pats her curlers. "Goodness, I didn't see you drive up."

Quentin looks at me and shakes his head. "Mom's taking Flash to yet another dog show."

"That would be Lord Flash Lightningstrike, sired by Lucky Louis of Kenmore." Mrs. Cole rubs behind Flash's ears. "Two-time champion."

Flash pants and drools, then perks up his ears at a distant squirrel.

"Just making a delivery," Mama says.

Mrs. Cole frowns. "I didn't order anything. Did I?"

Mama snatches the box from my clutches and hops out

of the Fireflite. "Actually, this was a gift ordered for Quentin."

"Wow!" Quentin takes the box. "From who?"

Mama smiles. "I can't say. A secret admirer."

I try very hard not to catch Quentin's eye.

"Thank you, ma'am."

I slide out of the Fireflite and pet Flash for the excuse of standing close to Quentin. Even though he's been tainted by Authelia.

Flash spits his drooly ball onto my sandals, and I jump back. "Hey!"

Quentin laughs. "He likes you."

My face burns, but I keep my eyes on the dog. "Are you a droolhound? Huh?" I scratch behind Flash's ear, and he squints with bliss.

"Oh, he's going to need another bath now," Mrs. Cole says. "He's a frightful mess."

Out of the corner of my eye, I see Quentin peeking into the pink box. An invisible fist clenches around my stomach. If Mama sees...

"We really must be going," Mama says. "Have a nice day, you two!"

"Goodbye!" Mrs. Cole runs after Flash again, who's decided to flee to the backyard.

Quentin waves at us, and I meet his eyes. How will he look at me the next time we meet? My twist my fingers in my lap. Mama gives the Fireflite some gas, and its engine purrs as we pull back onto the road.

Before the Cole house is even out of sight, Mama says, "Yes, it really is obvious."

"What is?" I say, trying to sound as cool as a cucumber.

She looks at me over the top on her sunglasses. "You and Quentin."

Forget cool. My face goes boiling hot. "What do you mean by a thing like that?"

"Sweetheart, there's always a point in the life of a young lady where she looks at boys and sees them differently than she did before."

I want to clap my hands over my ears. I'm about ready to die from mortification.

"Quentin certainly is a charming young man," Mama says, "for your first crush."

"Crush!" I squawk.

"Though," Mama says, "that's as far as it goes."

Suspicion coils in my belly. "Why?"

"Because we have secrets to keep." She doesn't need to say it. The unsaid words hang in the air. *Because we're witches.*

"Secrets everybody knows," I mutter.

Mama shoots me a glare. "So you told him?"

"No. Of course not!" I slump low in my seat. "And Mama, he's not my crush."

Mama just shakes her head and smiles, but it looks a little sad. And I understand why. Mr. and Mrs. Cole might smile at Quentin's oddball friend, but they would never let him date that witch with the twisted family tree.

"Mama?" I say. "Please don't drive so fast. I think I might be carsick."

She eases off the gas, even though we both know it's not her driving.

***

That evening, after Mama finishes washing up and I finish helping Daddy take out the trash, I sit at the kitchen table staring into a glass of water like I might find the secrets to the universe. Or at least myself.

"Josephine?" Mama trails downstairs in her dressing gown. "Honey, you can't still be carsick. Come upstairs."

"Not carsick." I force myself to gulp some water. "Just tired."

Mama rolls her eyes and puts her hand on my forehead. "Tired means bedtime."

I sigh. "Mama, I'm twelve. You don't need to baby me."

"You're always going to be my baby."

She squeezes me so tight my eyes bug. We hug for a little bit, me sitting, Mama standing.

"Don't you worry," Mama says, her voice muffled. "I'm sure you have a bright future ahead. You're my daughter, after all."

If only she knew what trouble I've been getting myself

into!

"Thanks, Mama. I think I might go to bed early now."

But I don't. As soon as she's preoccupied, I sneak out of the house.

I'm going to go wild waiting like this, not knowing.

My hands get all sweaty as I walk to Quentin's. Fireflies dust the trees like spilled glitter, and a cool-as-lemonade breeze lifts my hair from my neck. I'm finding the air thinner, for some reason. When I get to the Cole house, I'm lightheaded.

I rap on the door. Quentin answers it.

"Josephine!" He's got rumpled hair and a sleepy look of surprise in his eyes, like I just woke him up from a nap. "What time is it?"

My face heats. "Not too late, I hope. Were you sleeping?"

"No," he says. "Just watching *The Lone Ranger*."

He's being a couch potato? Maybe the conjure hasn't kicked in yet.

"You here to deliver something?" he says.

"What? No, that pie was it. As far as I know."

He shrugs, then smiles. "Too bad. I'd love an endless supply of desserts from a secret admirer." He pats his stomach and sighs like he's full. "So long as the desserts come from your mama, of course. She's a fantastic cook."

I try not to let my face crumple. Am I such a failure that I can't even bake one pie right? Or is this it?

Unforgettable friendship?

"Josephine?" His voice changes. "You okay?"

I plaster a smile on my face. "Actually, my mama wasn't the one who baked that pie."

"Oh?" He frowns. "Then who did?"

Lord, how oblivious can one boy be? And how hot can my cheeks go?

"I did," I say real quick. "That pie was all my idea." It's only half a lie.

Now he's blushing, too, his whole face red. "Why, thank you."

"You're welcome," I say.

He scratches the back of his head. "I thought you didn't bake."

"Which is why it probably wasn't any good, so I'm sorry I gave it to you, and—"

"I haven't eaten any yet."

"What? Why?"

He blinks at my outburst, then shrugs. "Saving it for after supper."

Simple as that. A laugh escapes me like a bubble popping.

"Would you like to come in?" he says.

I smile and try not to turn tail before he can even take a bite of my pie. In their fashionably avocado-colored living room, wallpapered by ribbons and rosettes won by Flash, Mr. and Mrs. Cole sit on the couch watching cowboys on TV. Flash snoozes between them, and he barely wags his tail at me. The smell of fried chicken and potatoes lingers in the air, and there's a folding table covered with throwaway aluminum trays. Those newfangled TV suppers—blasphemy, in the DeLune home.

"Josephine's here," Quentin says. "Mom? Dad?"

Mrs. Cole nudges Mr. Cole, who waves without looking up.

"Miss DeLune," Mrs. Cole says, "so nice to see you again." There's a sharpness in her voice and eyes as she watches Quentin and me.

I give her a big smile. "Hope I didn't interrupt your program."

"Oh, no, not at all!" She hesitates, then says, "Making a delivery at this hour?"

"Just doing a follow-up on an earlier delivery," I lie real quick. "A taste test."

Mrs. Cole flushes slightly. "For that pie?"

The way she says pie, with a little hitch in her voice, I can tell she read that article by Mr. Riley E. Bates, and is consequently very suspicious of black magic in homemade baked goods, especially DeLune ones. Quentin wasn't saving the pie for after supper; he probably hid it to keep his mother from throwing it out.

I bite the inside of my cheek. Why didn't I think of that earlier?

Quentin meets Mrs. Cole's eyes. "Josephine baked it.

I'm sure it's delicious."

At least Quentin's sweet enough to trust me. He thinks I'm not a witch, or that I'd never feed him conjure. Too bad I have to lie to him.

"All right!" Mrs. Cole titters a false laugh. "Enjoy the taste test, you two."

Quentin ushers me into the kitchen, muttering, "Sorry about that. She's being odd."

And I know why, but of course I don't tell him that.

I clasp my hands behind my back and try to breathe as he starts slicing the Forget-Me-Not Pie. Red juice bleeds beneath the blade, and I touch my thumb to the scab on my finger. When Quentin grabs two plates, I shake my head.

"I don't actually want to taste-test it," I say. "It's all for you."

"That's really sweet of you," he says, his ears crimson.

I nod and smile. Nobody else better eat that pie by accident.

Quentin sinks a fork into his slice and takes a bite.

He frowns, and his chewing slows. He swallows. "You sure you don't want any?"

I shake my head.

Forkful after forkful of Forget-Me-Not Pie disappears into his mouth. There's a clock on the wall, and with every tick my heartbeat slows. My face feels hot, then cold, like all the blood is draining out of it. I'm empty, exhausted, like I might slide to the floor any minute. I lean against the counter and try to look like it's on purpose.

Is this the conjure working, drawing upon my power?

Quentin spears the last cherry on his fork and eats it. He licks his lips.

"Was it good?" I say. I hope I sound normal. I can't tell.

"Delectable." He closes his eyes and breathes in slow. "Might I walk you home on this fine evening, Miss DeLune?"

When he says it, I hear a hint of something quivering and hopeful in his voice.

Wait. What does he mean? Is he joking?

"Yes, please," I say, and it comes out a bit breathless.

When I move away from the counter, I stumble a little, but he doesn't notice. We tiptoe out the back door, avoiding Mr. and Mrs. Cole, then step into the evening together. Quentin flicks on a flashlight, and little lost moths swirl into its beam. Blinded, they bump into the bulb, shimmering dust falling from their wings.

"Oh, poor moths," I say. "Turn it off. We can see good enough anyway."

Without a word, Quentin flicks off the light. We start walking along the path, slowly, my eyes still not ready for the dark.

"Aren't the fireflies pretty?" I say. "They remind me—"

"Josephine."

Quentin turns to me and closes the distance between

us. My heartbeat stumbles to a halt, then comes back harder than ever.

I touch his arm. "What is it?"

His skin burns beneath my fingertips, almost feverish, but I feel like the sick one.

"I might have said something earlier," he says, "that was wrong."

"Quentin, there are a great deal of things you might have said earlier that were wrong."

He laughs, then sobers again. "I'm serious. I'm talking about us being friends."

I feel like crickets are jittering in my ribcage. "You want to be enemies? That's fine with me." Lord, why can't I stop joking?

"Josephine." His eyes look silvery in the starlight. "Sometimes friends aren't good enough. I think I'm falling for you."

The bottom drops out from my stomach. "What did you just say?"

He gives me a tiny smile. "You heard me."

No, you're not supposed to say that! I didn't want this at all, I only wanted to keep you from falling for Authelia...

Be careful when measuring for this recipe, as it can be overpowering in a jiffy.

Oh.

He's falling for *me*. Before the conjure, or after? Maybe

he would have told me this, wanted to tell me this, before I fed him my magic and my blood, but now I will never know the truth. Because this isn't true love, and it's a far cry from friendship.

Sweet Jesus, what have I done?

He tries to hold me close, but I break free and run.

"Josephine!"

Quentin chases after me, his fingers closing on my wrist, but I yank away and keep running. My eyes burn with held-back tears. I'm faster than him, but only just, and it hurts to breathe. My ribs feel like iron bands.

"Josephine, stop." He catches me and tugs me around to face him. "Please."

I shake my head and blink hard. "I can't do this."

"I'm sorry," he says, his eyes so blue and earnest.

He's sorry, for what I've done.

I swallow hard. "Not your fault," I say. "You're so sweet, Quentin, I—"

A look of relief sweeps over his face, and he takes both of my hands in his. He's standing real close now, his eyes bright. "Might I...?"

He wants to kiss me.

The blood drains out of my face, then rushes back so hotly I might burn to ashes. Now I know for certain my conjure has gone wrong. This would be my first kiss, his first kiss, and now is too, too soon. It would be fake. Ruined.

Unforgettable friendship. That's all I wanted.

"Oh, Quentin," I say, and it's more sigh than words.

A man clears his throat, loudly.

Quentin and I both jump. We're right outside the porch of Mr. Glumphy, who's gnawing on a lump of chewing tobacco.

"That's downright wrong," Mr. Glumphy says.

"Excuse me?" I say.

Eyes blazing, Quentin says, "I don't think that's any of your business."

Mr. Glumphy spits some tobacco at us. "You're going to get yourself jinxed, boy."

While Quentin's still busy glaring at Mr. Glumphy, I run for it. He calls my name, but I'm already way ahead and almost home, even with my stupid dress catching around my knees and slowing me down.

"Josephine!" Quentin shouts. "I love you!"

I wince. Everybody within five blocks likely heard that.

I sprint into my backyard, charge up the front steps, and leap inside like the porch is made of lava. When I whirl around, I see Quentin running up the path. I can't quite bring myself to slam the door in his face, but—

"What's all that shouting about?" Cleon stands at the top of the staircase.

"Cleon!" I gasp. "It backfired. The—"

"Excuse me." Quentin hovers in the doorway, breathing hard. "Could I have a moment with you, Miss DeLune?"

I step onto the porch and shake my head. "Later."

Quentin starts to talk, but he's stopped by Cleon's big-eyed look. With a sigh, Quentin drops to one knee and grabs my hand. "Goodbye," he whispers.

I nod and pray real hard that he will leave me in peace.

Quentin climbs to his feet and jogs away, as if walking isn't good enough anymore, but he spares one last soulful glance at me.

This isn't the Quentin I know. And I'm not sure I'll ever see him that way again.

When he's out of sight, Cleon wolf-whistles. "Aren't you too young for a beau?"

I glare at him with all I've got, then sag against the porch railing and start laughing so hard tears escape my eyes. "My thoughts exactly."

"Sweet Jesus," Cleon says. "What kind of conjure did you feed that boy?"

Suddenly I'm not laughing anymore, just crying.

"Josephine?" My brother looks scared and angry, like he always does when I'm upset.

I shake my head. "I'm okay."

"What did he do to you? If he hurt you—"

"No. It's what I did to him."

Wobbly-kneed, I climb upstairs to my bedroom and go to bed early. Of course I can't sleep. I can't stop thinking of how close Quentin came to kissing me, or how he's never going to forgive me once he knows I'm a betrayer.

That night, after I fall asleep, or maybe before, Shaula stands by my pillow. Moonlight ripples across her skin, which glitters with as many stars as the Milky Way. She smiles at me, but I roll away from her and stare at the ceiling.

"What's the matter, *ma chère*?" she says. "You cooked some wonderful conjure."

"I didn't want what I got," I say.

She's silent for a moment. "You won Quentin."

I swallow hard. "Won him? I wanted him as a friend. Not... like that."

"And you know this how?"

The hint of scorn in her voice makes me glare at her. "The way he was acting wasn't Quentin at all. I know him better than that."

Shadows thicken around Shaula. "Does it matter?"

"Of course it does."

Her hair tangles in an unearthly wind. "You will not pine over a foolish dream of friendship. You are a witch of my own blood, Josephine, and I have not lingered this long to watch the Ravenous One devour you."

I slide out of bed and straighten, my fists clenched at my sides. "Did I say that?"

"You must take the bitter with the sweet. Conjure is

never without consequences."

"Fine." My face blazes. "But you're dead wrong if you think I'm swooning around and waiting to be eaten alive. I don't like what my conjure did to Quentin, but I know I have to keep trying until I can control myself better."

Shaula arches an eyebrow. "And what will you do now?"

"Cook up some more conjure. Any suggestions?"

A thin smile spreads on her lips. "Nothing is more delicious than revenge."

EIGHT

O ur neighbors the Ralstons have this ancient barn that looks like it shipwrecked on the rocks by our backyard—every year it sinks deeper into a green sea of weeds. The Ralstons don't use it for nothing, so it's a perfect place to be alone.

I sit on the cool dirt floor and glance at the slivers of heaven in the roof. Looks like an afternoon storm might be rolling in. I'd better hurry.

I already know who's going to taste my revenge.

I drag Grandma Lula's cookbook onto my lap. It's heavier than I remembered, and bigger than the Bible. As I open the book, its leather spine creaks a complaint. Oddly enough, the order of the recipes looks different this time. There's no 'Charlotte's Own Sweet Rice' or 'Persnickety Pastries' anymore, or at least I can't find them. Instead, I discover bad luck dumplings and wickedness-fried chicken. Definitely dark conjure.

GREAT-AUNT GILLIE'S GREEN TOMATO PIE

An economical way to use unripe tomatoes and ruin an enemy's day in a most satisfying manner. The piquant flavor of the tomatoes does wonders to disguise the taste of bad luck. Guaranteed to give anyone a hard time. Be careful not to mix with any good luck ingredients, as that can produce calamitous results.

Bad luck would certainly be an interesting revenge, though I doubt Authelia would come within ten feet of a green tomato pie. She calls that sort of thing "poor man's food," and hates vegetables besides. Lord, how am I going to get her to eat my conjure? It's going to have to be one of her favorites, delivered with clever trickery.

"What's this?" I mutter.

DEVIL'S OWN DILL PICKLES

Heavenly dill pickles, spiced with devilish vengeance. Made-to-order humiliations for your enemies. Quickening salt speeds pickling process from two weeks to two days. Add ingredients of your revenge on the first night; serve after the second.

Authelia *loves* pickles. Perfect! I can sneak some Devil's Own Dill Pickles into her next burger at Carl and Earl's when she comes to sneer at me.

I read the list of ingredients out loud. "Cukes, pickling salt, dill... where's the conjure?"

I lean my head back against the barn wall. Maybe "made-to-order" means I have to pick the ingredients myself? I study the recipe with more care, and notice a note scribbled into the margins.

GOOD: *rotten mushrooms, hair from a sick dog, newt slime.*
BAD: *ashes from a burnt-down house, grave dust.*

Does "BAD" mean that the ingredients didn't work, or that they worked so powerfully that the poor soul who ate this conjure received some horrible revenge? *Grave dust.* I shudder. Somebody in my family went deep into the darkness.

I trade Grandma Lula's cookbook for my grimoire. The battered old cover doesn't even say "Dictionary" anymore, but there's no use pretending. I try not to flinch as I pry it open. At first, the pages look faded, almost blank. Then words wriggle up toward me like black goldfish in a pond, begging for food. Almost friendly.

I poke one of the words—*chandelier*—and it wiggles beneath my fingertip, nibbling at my skin in a tingly sort of way.

"Sorry," I say, "but I doubt I'll be needing any

chandeliers for this recipe."

The word darts away, disappearing into the crack between the pages. Another dozen words swarm around my finger.

"Are you alive?" I say, and then I feel dumb for talking to a book.

A word floats to the top of the page. *Yes.*

My heart does a funny little leap. "Good lord. Shaula, are you in there?"

The words swirl around, but don't make any sense. Maybe that's not how this grimoire thing works. Mama just jots down notes in hers, with a plain ballpoint pen, but who knows what she does when I'm not looking.

I rummage in my pocket for a pencil. In careful, purposeful letters, I write:

Ingredients For Revenge
maybe rotten mushrooms

The penciled-in words darken to black, as if they'd been printed there all along. When I try to erase "maybe rotten mushrooms," the words flee beyond the edge of the page and don't come back. I'd better be careful what I write!

A fat raindrop plops on my head. I look up just in time for two more to slip through the roof and land on my cheeks like tears. I shut my grimoire with a *whomp* and snatch up Grandma Lula's cookbook. With both books

tucked under my arms, I run out of the Ralstons' barn
while the rain swells from a trickle to a downpour.

Halfway into our backyard, I kick up a nail lying in the
grass. Twisted and useless. I pick it up and weigh it in my
palm.

It *feels* right.

I pocket it. And then I make a note in my grimoire.

***

Mama doesn't have any cukes in the fridge—believe it or
not, it isn't bottomless—so as soon as the rain slows to
drippy-faucet speed, I hop on my bike and pedal into
Paris. In the parking lot of the Higgledy-Piggledy
Supermarket, the skin on the back of my neck prickles,
like somebody's following me.

I sneak a quick glance around, but the street looks
empty. No, wait—there's a tan-colored meteor hurtling
nearer. A greyhound by the name of Flash. I climb off my
bike, and he catches up with me, panting and whimpering.

"What is it, boy?" I say.

Flash wags his tail so hard his whole behind shakes. He
jumps on me and almost knocks me over, licking my cheek
with his hot tongue.

"Is it Quentin? Is he in trouble?"

Flash just stares at me with his dark eyes, then whines,
his ears vibrating. I push his paws off my shoulders, then

sit on the sidewalk. He lays his head in my lap and snuggles up against me. For a dog who couldn't care less about me the last time I saw him, he's being *really* friendly... like he licked a certain pie dish clean.

I groan. "I'm sorry, boy. You've been eating things you shouldn't."

He barks, and trots alongside me. As I open the door to the Higgledy-Piggledy, he almost squeezes past my legs, but I shove him back.

"No, Flash," I say. "Stay."

Flash droops, still wagging his tail hopefully.

"Go home. You know Quentin's going to miss you. And Mrs. Cole isn't going to be too happy if you skip one of those dog shows."

He lies down on the sidewalk, his nose between his paws, and sighs. Poor dog.

My hair sticks to my sweaty forehead, no matter how many times I brush it back, and my mouth feels dryer than sandstone. I step into the air-conditioned heaven of the Higgledy-Piggledy and breathe a sigh of blessed relief.

I load up my basket with cucumbers, then detour to the freezers, hungry for cold. Ice cream, more ice cream, popsicles. Hang on. What's this? Frozen cheesecake, pastries, and ready-to-go biscuit dough. I've never seen these before! Must be some new scientific invention. All the boxes are labeled with swirly red letters.

"McArthur Mills. Homemade Taste. Factory Quality

You Can Trust."

I feel like I swallowed a lump of ice. They aren't just selling flour anymore. They're treading into DeLune territory.

I slam the freezer door shut, but the strawberry cheesecake taunts me with a perfectly photographed slice on the box. I glance around the Higgledy-Piggledy, since I'd rather die than let anyone see me, then grab the strawberry cheesecake and tuck it under my arm. I creep out of that aisle like I'm on a top-secret mission.

Right as the lady at the checkout rings up my total, the front doors open. Of all the people who could walk in, it has to be Authelia. I stuff the frozen cheesecake into a paper bag before Authelia can see her last name plastered all over the product and know what a horrible traitor I am. No, not a traitor—a spy, doing reconnaissance.

"Oh, hello," Authelia says, all but rolling her eyes at me.

I look sideways at her. "Uh-huh."

Authelia's wearing a beautiful dress in robin's egg blue, the full skirt bordered with hydrangea flowers, with daring gold pumps. Raindrops glitter in her hair like diamonds. My stomach clenches. She better not be making an extra effort to lure Quentin away from me. Not after my Forget-Me-Not Pie fiasco.

"That'll be a dollar eighty nine," the checkout lady says to me.

I dig out my money with sweaty hands, praying I have enough.

"What are you buying?" Authelia says airily.

"Food."

This time Authelia does roll her eyes. "I'm not blind." She pauses, then looks at the checkout lady. "What aisle do you keep the pineapple in?"

The checkout lady snaps her gum. "Honey, we have canned pineapple in aisle three."

Authelia sighs in this incredibly jaded way. "Canned pineapple? Not fresh? We're having a Hawaiian pool party next Saturday."

Pool party? Authelia flashes me a grin, and I stand there steaming like a lobster in a pot.

"Sorry." The checkout lady shrugs. "But I hear Dole makes decent canned."

"All right! I guess that will have to do." Authelia saunters off to aisle three.

Oh, that's right. Gossip says Authelia and the rest of the McArthurs are jetting to Hawaii for a vacation later this summer. Guess this pool party is practice for lounging around under palm trees and nibbling on exotic fruits.

Face hot, I pay the checkout lady and high-tail it out of the Higgledy-Piggledy.

I almost trip over Flash on the way out, and he starts whimpering. "Go home, Flash."

He lowers his head and looks up at me with soulful

eyes.

"Go home!" I point in the general direction of Quentin's house. "Come on, go home!"

Flash whines and pushes his head against my hand, licking my fingers, then leans his long body against my legs. I sigh and pat him on the head. I never did think Mrs. Cole trained him to do anything besides dog shows.

I zoom out of there on my bike, but it's pretty pointless to try outrunning a greyhound. Flash lopes alongside me, panting, his mouth open in a happy dog grin. As soon as I get home, I park my bike and dart through the back door. Flash isn't quick enough to follow me, and he starts whimpering and pawing at the porch.

"Lord, you'd better not scratch that paint!" I mutter.

I smuggle everything from the Higgledy-Piggledy into my bedroom. The cucumbers look fine, if a bit bruised, but the cheesecake defrosted itself. I dart downstairs, grab a fork from the kitchen, and run back up, my heart pounding.

"Josephine!" Cleon lurks at the top of the stairs. "You trying to put out an eye?"

"Um, no," I say, a little out of breath. "And could you let me past?"

Cleon leans against the wall to block my way. "What's the fork for?"

I gnaw on the inside of my cheek. Should I tell him? Even though he wins the blue ribbon for being annoying, he's never broken a promise or spilled a secret. And maybe he can give me a second opinion on this cheesecake catastrophe.

"Follow me," I say, trying to sound all sure of myself.

"Uh-oh," he says. "You've been baking again?"

"Not me." I lower my voice. "McArthur Mills."

"What?" His eyebrows go sky-high. "What do you mean?"

I fling open my bedroom door and nudge him inside. The cheesecake sits in its box on my dresser, drops of melted freezer frost sliding down the pretty photograph. Cleon whistles low under his breath, then pries open the box.

There it is—the enemy's baking.

A cheesecake as white as first snow, with strawberries glistening like rubies, sits on a perfectly round crust of graham cracker crumbs.

"I'm sure it tastes horrible," I say. "Like toothpaste and stale bread."

"It certainly doesn't look horrible," Cleon says.

"Let's try it."

I cut out a forkful of tender, quivery cheesecake and pop it into my mouth with a grimace. A deliciously rich sweetness spreads over my tongue, like eating clouds honeyed in sunlight. It tingles a little bit in the back of my throat.

"That..." I swallow. "That tastes like conjure."

Cleon snatches the fork from me, even though it has my germs on it, and takes a bite. His eyes get buggy. "Like *Mama's* conjure."

We both look at the cheesecake.

"Are you going to tell her?" I say.

"Me?" Cleon grabs the cheesecake box and stares at the back. "Heck no." He pauses. "The ingredients don't say anything about conjure."

I laugh a hollow laugh. "Why would they? 'Beware of Baked Black Magic.'"

Cleon's eyebrows descend. He stares at the cheesecake real hard, then closes the box with quick fingers and picks the whole thing up.

"What are you doing?" I say.

"Getting rid of the evidence," he says. "Mama has enough to worry about already."

"But what about—"

He fixes me with a frown. "She's going to find out sooner or later, and it doesn't have to be from us. We can't make this any less worse than it already is."

I suppose he's right, but the cheesecake's terribly delicious taste lingers on my tongue.

***

Come suppertime, Mama returns home with a basketful of hot cornbread and chicken.

"You all better be hungry," she says. "I brought old Mrs. Welsummer some of my Special Spiced Plums today, and after she gossiped my ear off for a good hour or two, she insisted on paying me with her own cooking."

"Cornbread smells good!" Cleon says brightly. "I'll set the table."

"I'll help," I say.

I grab the napkins and catch my brother's eye. He raises his eyebrows and nods. I don't see a crumb of the frozen cheesecake, which means he must have eaten with the evidence with his bottomless stomach. I give him a quick thumb's up.

Daddy saunters through the back door not more than a minute later. "I'm home!"

"I can see that." Mama bustles around the kitchen. "Hurry and wash up, supper's ready!"

As soon as we all settle down and start to eat, Flash scratches on the front door. I grit my teeth and keep a poker face.

"What's that commotion?" Daddy swallows his chicken. "One of those raccoons?"

"Hope not," Cleon says cheerfully. "Those things carry all sorts of infectious diseases."

Mama stabs her fork into her cornbread. Grumbling, she starts to stand.

"It's not a raccoon," I say quickly. "It's Quentin's dog. He followed me home."

"You mean that greyhound?" Mama sinks back into her chair, but her eyes are still narrowed. "Mrs. Cole pampers that dog to death."

"I hope something *bad* didn't happen to Quentin." Cleon waggles his eyebrows.

I kick my brother under the table.

Mama's gaze slides between the two of us. She's got a nose for trouble.

Flash whimpers and scratches harder on the door. I wince and hope he's not leaving claw marks. When is that Forget-Me-Not Pie going to wear off?

"That does it." Mama rises to her feet and grabs a pitcher of water.

The cornbread sticks in my throat, and I swallow hard.

Mama sweeps open the front door. Flash barks and hops, thinking he's going to be let inside, but she dumps the pitcher of water on him. The poor dog yelps like he's been scalded and shoots out of there with his tail between his legs.

Mama shuts the door, refills the pitcher in the kitchen, and settles back down. "There."

I pretend to be too bored and tired to say anything else on the subject, and shovel cornbread into my mouth as fast as manners will allow. I get through the rest of supper without a hitch, then excuse myself and get ready for bed. Night falls like a black blanket, swift and sudden, with pinprick holes for stars. I'm just about ready to tug up the sheets when I hear, right outside my window, an earsplitting howl.

I dash to the window and slide it open. "Flash!"

Flash barks and wiggles, then drops into a playful bow, like I'm going to throw a ball for him at this ungodly hour. I glare at him and start to shut the window, but he throws back his head and looses another one of those banshee wails. Lights in the neighbors' houses start flicking on. I growl and run outside in my nightie.

"What are you still doing here?" I whisper.

The greyhound leaps on me and slobbers all over my hands.

I sigh. "You want to stay with me?"

He woofs.

And so he does, sleeping curled at the foot of my bed and taking up more space than should be possible for one skinny, prize-winning greyhound. He would make a pretty good foot-warmer—if it wasn't the middle of summer. I kick off my sheets and earn myself a glare from Flash, who's decided this bed belongs to him, just like I do. At last, we reach an agreement about who's getting what part of the bed, and I nod off.

Only to be woken by a low growl, and a strange shadow on the wall.

NINE

Flash crouches on my bed, his body shaking. I blink and rub my eyes.

The shadow stretches across the wall by my window, a tangle of angles like the old catalpa tree outside, swaying in the wind. But it dawns on me that those shadows should be *behind* me, judging by the slant of the moonlight.

The Ravenous One.

My breath snags in my throat. The shadows creep across my bedroom, fingers fumbling in the dark. I leap off my bed and switch on the overhead light. The Ravenous One jets backward like a startled octopus and darts through my open window. I slam the window shut before he can turn around and sneak back inside.

Flash lunges from my bed, brave now that the threat is good and gone, and sniffs furiously along the floorboards.

I rub the goosebumps on my arms like I can erase them. "Flash. Come here, boy."

The greyhound thrusts his nose toward the window, his body all streamlined and silhouetted like one of those comic book superheroes, growls for good measure, then hops back onto my bed and curls up in my sheets.

Lord, that was close. I'm leaving that window shut, never mind the sweltering heat.

Still jumpy, I chew on a hangnail and think for a second. Mama says she hung a witch ball over my crib when I was a baby, and I still have it somewhere. That kind of warding conjure would certainly be nice to have. I walk over to my closet and start rummaging through boxes. Flash lifts his head, his ears perked, and watches.

Tucked in old newspapers in a shoebox, I find it.

The witch ball is a globe of rich aquamarine glass, about the size of a Christmas ornament, with threads of glass spiderwebbing inside—and just like a spiderweb, the threads can catch dark conjure as if it's nothing more than an unlucky bottle fly. There's a leather cord threaded through the top of the witch ball, so I hang it on an old nail over my window. Moonlight gleams through the glass.

"See?" I tell Flash. "That witch ball should keep us safe. Well, safer at least."

The greyhound makes a high whine that turns into a yawn.

"There's also peppermint," I say. "That's supposed to

ward off voodoo spirits, though it might just ward off ants in the pantry."

I tiptoe barefoot out of my room and creep into the kitchen. Flash pads after me, his claws clicking on the linoleum, and I pray we don't wake anybody. In the window over the sink, Shaula walks into sight. She mouths my name, then beckons me with her hand. I swallow hard and grab a flashlight from a drawer.

"Stay close, Flash," I mutter.

I open the back door and step into the scent of rainy earth and the chorusing of crickets.

"Josephine," whispers a voice on the wind.

Like a drop of ink in water, Shaula swirls into being beside me. Her skin shimmers under the starlight, and her hair stirs gently in a wind that doesn't belong to this world. Flash woofs and jumps back, his ears flattened against his skull.

"Is the Ravenous One out here?" I whisper, my mouth dry.

Shaula shakes her head. "You saw his shadow, since he was not yet ready to enter this realm. But now he knows where you sleep at night."

I shudder, even though it's nearly eighty degrees out here.

Shaula glances at my bedroom window. "Your witch ball is a quaint superstition."

"Oh?" My stomach plummets. "You mean it's useless?"

She tilts her head to one side, then nods.

"What's to keep the Ravenous One from eating me in my sleep?"

Shaula looks at me, her eyes swimming with stars. "Me."

"Great," I mutter. "That makes me feel so much better."

Flash paces behind me, jittery, and presses his cold nose to my hand.

"Your dog may help as well," Shaula says. "Certain animals have a talent for sniffing out conjure before humans can."

I make a face. "He's not my dog. I'm only borrowing him."

Shaula isn't listening, her gaze fixed on the sky. "Tonight is a perfect night for you to cook your conjure. Are you ready?"

"Nearly," I say. "Well, I need a few more ingredients…"

Shaula starts fraying around the edges. "I will wait for you."

And she dissolves into the night.

***

Far after my bedtime, while Mama and Daddy are still snoring, I sweep the beam of my flashlight around the Ralstons' barn, just to make sure I have the place to myself. The smell of alfalfa hangs in the air. Alfalfa, and vinegar.

I shine my flashlight on a low rafter. By the sickly yellow glow, the cucumbers soaking in their pickling jar look like zombie vegetables. From my backpack, I take out my ingredients. One twisted, rusted old nail. One crow's eggshell, nearly whole. A five-leaf clover, one too many leaves to be lucky. A broken cat's claw.

Flash sniffs the cat's claw and growls low in his throat.

I peer into the darkness. "Shaula? I'm ready."

Shaula swirls into being beside me, and Flash slinks away to go lie down by the door.

I take a shuddery breath and unscrew the lid of the pickling jar—counterclockwise, of course. Dark conjure always has to be backwards from the light stuff, otherwise it can be a powerful dangerous mix-up of magic.

Fingers quivering, I pick up the twisted nail. "Here's what I found."

With feather-soft fingers, Shaula slips the twisted nail from my hand.

"Strong conjure." Her eyes glimmer. "You have chosen well."

Pride stirs from its perch in my heart. I yank my hair from its ponytail and shake it out so my curls hang wild and witch-like around my face.

"Thank you," I say. "I picked that because it felt... twisted."

Shaula nods, unsmiling. "Who do you intend it for?"

"My friend," I say. "*Ex*-friend."

Heat creeps into my cheeks. It's strange, telling her these sort of personal things. Even though I suppose we're technically family. And she technically knows a lot more about me than I ever would care to tell her.

"Which will you add first?" Shaula says.

I hadn't thought of that. I chew on the inside of my cheek. "Give me a second."

Slowly, I set the ingredients before me. The glare of the flashlight seems too bright, so I click it off. My eyes slide into nighttime seeing, and I study how the cat's claw gleams, how the crow's egg looks like a false gemstone.

An idea sneaks into my mind. I lug my grimoire from my backpack and lay it flat on a wooden box. The pages shine bright in a moonbeam, the words squiggling in curlicues. I flip to the page where I wrote down the list of ingredients I wanted. Sure enough, the very first ingredient on the list is *twisted nail*. I honestly can't remember what order I wrote these in, or if they maybe sorted themselves in my absence.

"This," I say, and I drop the nail into the pickling jar.

The nail sinks into the vinegar, trailing sparks like a shooting star. *Blue* sparks. I lean closer and watch the sparks fade. Shaula arches her eyebrow, but says nothing. A sweat breaks out on my forehead. What happens if I guessed wrong?

"Here goes nothing," I say, and I pick up the five-leafed

clover.

I purse my lips and drop the five-leaf clover into the pickles. It sizzles—*sizzles!*—when it hits the vinegar and dissolves into a froth of green. The fizzling pops and pricks in my nose. It stinks like acid eating into metal.

"Wow." I fan the air in front of my nose. "My eyes are watering!"

Flash sniffs the air, then sneezes explosively.

Shaula hovers behind me, smiling. "And next?"

I slide my finger down the page in my grimoire. "Cat's claw. Then crow's egg."

The claw plops into the vinegar and seesaws to the bottom, where it seeps into a dark blur that disappears. The egg shatters into a thousand sparkling pieces, as pretty as a waterfall of fireflies, and I can't help but laugh at this magic of my own making.

Shaula's hand falls, a shadow of a touch, on my shoulder. "Josephine."

My laughter dies in my throat with a strangled little sound. "What? Did I—?"

"Wonderful." Her voice is as plush and dark as a black cat. "You have such talent."

Talent.

The word sends a lightning spider crawling down my spine. It makes me want to leap and whoop and crow to the world that I am Josephine DeLune, and I am indeed a witch to be reckoned with. Mama never thought I was good enough to cook conjure, but Grandma Lula was right all along. She'd be so proud to see me now.

I take a deep swig of air thick with magic.

"One more night," I say, "I can harvest the fruits of my conjure. Well, vegetables."

Shaula's laugh drips with wildflower honey. "*Magnifique.*"

"The Devil's Own Dill Pickles." I grin. "My revenge."

***

When me and Flash trot down to breakfast the next day, both groggy and a bit twitchy, Mama glares at us.

"What's that hound doing in here?" she says.

"Flash howled outside my bedroom window until I let him in."

"Humph." Mama slaps a pancake over on the griddle. "Better be the only thing you let into your bedroom at night, young lady."

"Mama!" I wail.

Cleon gives me a look that says he can't believe it, either.

Flash's nose twitches, and he stares mesmerized at the griddle, his tail swinging slowly.

Daddy clomps downstairs and stops short in the doorway. "Hey, boy!" He pats Flash on the head. "So are we keeping him?"

Mama rolls her eyes. "Laurent, how about you bring him back to the Cole family today?"

"Sorry," Daddy says. "Got to get to work right after breakfast. Josephine?"

I sigh. "I'll do it." Never mind that my stomach feels like it's tying itself into knots.

Flash whines and paws at the linoleum. Mama gives him a look, then tosses him a hushpuppy she'd been frying out of leftover pancake batter.

"Time to eat!" Mama slides plates onto the table, each teetering with a tower of pancakes.

There's a knock on the door, so I answer it. Quentin stands there in the rain, his hair sparkling with water. My body feels tingly and faraway, like the time I flicked off the bathroom light with wet hands and got zapped on accident.

"What are you doing here?" I clear my throat and try to sound less rude. "You look wet."

He smiles, but it's kind of sad. "I'm looking for Flash. Have you seen him anywhere?"

My face gets hot. "He followed me home last night, and… well…" I open the front door wider, so he can see into the kitchen.

Flash lies under the kitchen table, gnawing on the hushpuppy.

"Oh, whew." Quentin whistles and slaps his thighs. "Flash! Come here, boy!"

The greyhound blinks.

Daddy grabs Flash by his collar and tugs. "Come on, dog, time for you to go home."

The greyhound spreads his legs, his claws scrabbling on the linoleum, and makes a high-pitched whine. He gives me a pitiful look.

"Wait a sec." Quentin digs in his pocket and pulls out a sock tied in a knot. A really nasty, slimy old thing that looks like it's been drooled on one too many times. He dangles it in the doorway. "Look, Flash. Your favorite!"

Flash looks at the sock, then nibbles his hushpuppy.

Mama glances over her shoulder. "Quentin, honey, I don't think your dog is likely to budge for the time being, not with that hushpuppy, so you'd best join us for a bit of breakfast. Come out of the rain and grab a plate."

"Thanks, Mrs. DeLune," Quentin says, "but no thanks."

Mama looks him up and down. "Did you have breakfast already?"

"No, but—"

"You're starting to look skinny. There're plenty of pancakes to go around."

Both Quentin and I blush, me out of sympathy.

"Well," he says, "I suppose I could have just one pancake."

"That's more like it," Mama says, and loads up a plate with three.

Quentin takes off his coat, shakes off the rainwater,

then steps inside. His arm knocks against mine, and my heartbeat flutters.

"Sorry," he says to me.

His eyes meet mine, somehow a deeper blue than usual. I get the distinct feeling that he's not just apologizing about bumping into me.

"So how's your summer been, Quentin?" Daddy says.

"Good," Quentin says, but his eyes look forlorn.

I take a deep swig of cold orange juice in the hopes that it will cool my blazing cheeks. Cleon keeps glancing at me and waggling his eyebrows, until I kick him square in the shin. Mama and Daddy don't notice, too busy eating their pancakes, and neither does Quentin, too busy gazing at my face. Flash, however, growls. He's looking pretty protective of that hushpuppy between his paws.

"*What* is that *sock* doing in the kitchen?" Mama says.

Flash's so-called favorite toy lies in front of Quentin, who snatches it up and stuffs it into his pocket. "Sorry, ma'am," he says.

"Bad enough having animals in here," Mama mutters. "You'd better wash your hands!"

But she slips Flash another hushpuppy when she thinks nobody's looking. Quentin takes an eternity washing his hands, then sits beside me. Cleon grabs the gooseberry jam and starts slathering it on his pancakes. I offer the syrup to Quentin, who takes it with a polite smile. My stomach tightens, and I can't look him in the eye.

We don't talk much as we finish up breakfast. I keep my eyes on making a swirly pattern with my syrup. Daddy kisses Mama goodbye and heads off to work, and then Quentin helps me carry the dirty dishes to the sink.

"Why, thank you, Quentin!" Mama says. "Such manners."

Quentin gives her a small smile. "I wonder if I might have a word with Josephine?"

Mama looks at me, her eyebrows raised, and says, "Why don't you ask her?"

I'm about ready to die of shame.

"Josephine?" He looks at me with his face red from his hairline to his neck.

"Sure!" I sound a lot more chipper than I feel. "How about the porch?"

"The porch?" Quentin shrugs. "Why not inside?"

Good lord, he better not confess his love to me right here and now!

"It's a nice day." I glance out the window and lie faster. "Look, it's not raining as hard."

"Still seems pretty wet to me."

"But I love the smell of rain."

I drag the oblivious boy with me before he can poke more holes in my excuses. It does smell delicious out here. My stomach, on the other hand, feels about as upset as the windblown dish-rag clouds streaming across the sky.

The screen door creaks shut behind us, and we sit on

the back porch.

I clear my throat. Now no words are coming out.

Quentin fumbles in his pocket. "Here." His face is still red. "For you."

He drops a necklace into my hand, a silver chain with a sweet little cockatiel charm, yellow celluloid, about the size of a quarter.

"It's a Crackerjack charm," he says, with a proud smile, "from my collection."

"From your collection?" I touch my fingers to my mouth. "Oh, I can't take this!"

He still looks so stubbornly hopeful. "I'm going to give it to you anyway, and I'm going to apologize for being so stupid."

My stomach twists up into a knot. "Quentin…"

He takes a deep breath, and his cheeks turn even redder, if at all possible. "I know you think I'm crazy, and I said a lot of crazy things, but I still want to be friends if you can maybe ignore what happened that night."

"No."

"No?" Quentin's face falls. "Why?"

"You don't need to apologize." I force myself to meet his eyes. "That wasn't your fault."

"What—what do you mean?"

I clench the Crackerjack charm in my hand. "Remember that pie I brought you?"

"The one with the cherries?"

I nod and twist my toes inside my sandals. "That was a Forget-Me-Not Pie. I baked it myself, just for you, but it backfired."

"Oh." He ducks his head. "I figured that pie had conjure in it."

"What?" I stare at him. "And you still ate it?"

"I figured it couldn't be *bad* conjure," he mutters, "since you gave it to me."

"Quentin!" I smack myself on the forehead. "You can't just go around eating conjure. The only reason I baked that Forget-Me-Not Pie in the first place was because Authelia ordered a Sweetheart Pie for you, and I swapped them."

"Authelia?" Quentin wrinkles his nose. "What does a Sweetheart Pie do?"

I roll my eyes. "Good lord, use your imagination."

He sticks out his tongue. "Well, I'm glad I ate your pie instead."

"But I told you, it didn't work." My face burns. "I only wanted us to stay friends."

"Oh." Quentin rubs the back of his neck. "That's okay with me."

But the Crackerjack charm in my hand says otherwise. I sit there feeling like a complete fool, my eyes stinging, and try not to cry.

"I'm real sorry," I say. "You must think I'm a bad person and a worse witch."

He looks sideways at me, his eyes unreadable. "Well…"

I swallow hard, my throat aching. "You'd better take Flash home."

Quentin jumps to his feet like he was waiting for an excuse. We both head back into the kitchen, where all I can do is fake a smile and nod as he says goodbye. Nobody seems to notice that I'm not saying a word. Quentin finally lures Flash out from under the table, and then I watch both of them walk away in the rain.

TEN

The rain keeps falling in silver streaks for a day and a night, and then finally the sun sails out on an absolutely gorgeous afternoon. Dollops of whipped-cream clouds float in blue sky while I bike to Carl and Earl's.

"Daddy?" I say sweetly. "Can I help out?"

"Of course, Jo." Daddy tosses me an apron. "It's a pretty day for a pretty girl to carhop."

I roll my eyes and tie on the apron, then tug on my skates and coast out of there. Lauralee's working today, along with a few other carhops who never pay me much mind. I smile and wave at Lauralee, though.

"That friend of yours was here earlier," she says, twisting her hair into a ponytail.

"Friend?" My stomach tightens. "Who?"

"*You* know." Lauralee nudges me in the ribs. "The cute towheaded boy." She skates off with a platter of burgers.

Quentin. I blush hotter than the surface of the sun. After yesterday, of course he would look for me. I touch the yellow cockatiel charm at my neck, which I haven't had the heart to squirrel away in my jewelry box.

I skate after Lauralee. "Did he say if he was coming back?"

"So you *do* like him," she singsongs. "I knew it!"

"Lauralee," I groan.

She pretends to pout. "Don't worry about him. He'll come back, they always do." She skates away again, showing off with a little twirl.

"Thanks," I mutter, "I guess."

I meander around Carl and Earl's, tidying up trash, and keep a lookout for Quentin.

"I'm winning!" screams an all-too-familiar voice.

I loop back and stare.

Authelia's pedaling hard on a candy-apple red bike, two girls panting behind her. The three of them race straight toward me. Are they *trying* to run me over? As I swerve to the right, Authelia whooshes past me, her laughter on the wind.

"Oh my god, Authelia!" whines one of the girls. "You had a head start."

"Yeah, right." Still laughing, Authelia jumps off her bike and props it on its kickstand. "You're just a loser, Patsy."

"*You're* just a loser," Patsy repeats, mocking her. She

tightens her high blonde ponytail—bottle blonde, not like Authelia's.

The third of them, a tall brunette, coasts to a stop and gives me a cool once-over. "Hey."

I give her a once-over right back. She has amazingly green eyes, diamond studs in her ears, and a silver bike she leans on like it's a prize racehorse. I don't know her name, but I don't need to. She's one of *them*, the popular girls.

"Beverly, I'm starving." Authelia saunters over. "Oh, lucky us! Here's a carhop."

Her breathy voice instantly gets on my nerves, but I put on a fake smile. "Welcome back to Carl and Earl's, Authelia. The usual?"

"The usual?" Beverly glances at Authelia. "How often do you eat fast food?"

Authelia's cheeks turn pink. "Whenever I feel like it."

Patsy giggles. "But the carhop knows your name."

"Oh, wait," Beverly says, with a sly smile. "Is this *her*?"

Do I even want to know what trash Authelia has been talking about me?

I give this Beverly girl a hard look. "I'm right here. No need for the third person."

"Third person?" Patsy says, puzzled. "But there are four of us here…"

Authelia bursts out laughing. "Oh my god, Patsy, you're so stupid! She meant third person like the grammar third person."

Patsy scoffs and rolls her eyes. "Like I care!"

Beverly's still staring at me with this blank interest in her eyes, like a cat watching a goldfish. "So you're the one whose mom is a witch."

All the blood drains from my face.

Authelia gasps and throws her hands over her mouth. "You did not just say that!"

Patsy looks genuinely worried. "Guys! Not so loud. My parents would kill me if they heard us talking about— well, you know."

Beverly looks at her. "What, voodoo? It's not profanity." She sounds so confident.

I swallow hard and decide to play dumb. "Well, if you aren't ordering anything today, I'd better start helping paying customers..."

"Hold on," Beverly says. "We're ready now. Authelia?"

Authelia has uncertainty written all over her face. "I'll have the—the cheeseburger. But no fries. And extra pickles."

Extra pickles. Excellent.

"So, the usual," I say, with a perfectly innocent smile. "Coming right up."

Authelia's cheeks turn pink again, and she can't look me in the eye.

"I'll have a corndog?" Patsy says, her voice kind of squeaky. "And a coke?"

"Sure thing." I scribble down their orders. "And you?"

Beverly thinks for a moment. "I'll have what Authelia's having."

"Will do," I say.

I skate away and leave the three of them talking. I don't need to hear their words to know that they're gossiping about me and Mama.

As soon as I get the corndog and two cheeseburgers, I do a quick swap behind the kitchen. I eat Authelia's plain old pickles myself, then slip four crinkle-cut slices of the Devil's Own Dill Pickles into her burger instead.

There's still Beverly's cheeseburger. Well, I didn't slice enough Devil's Pickles for that.

I skate back to the three girls and make my delivery with a smile. None of them smile back. They carry their food to a picnic table.

"I'm not sure I'm hungry anymore." Patsy pokes at her corndog like it might be alive.

Beverly rolls her eyes. "Don't be a wimp. It's not a voodoo corndog." She takes a dainty bite of her burger.

Authelia dissects her burger. She peels off the lettuce and eats it, then the tomatoes. Finally, she reaches the Devil's Own Dill Pickles. Her face empty, she pops the pickles into her mouth, one by one, until she has eaten all of my conjure.

Now all I need to do is wait for my revenge.

The next morning brings a commotion in the kitchen. I crawl out of bed, blinking away dreams of pickles, and tug a dressing gown over my nightie. My clock says it's nearly eight, but I could swear it feels two hours earlier.

I trudge downstairs and step into the kitchen. "Mama?"

She bends over the oven and whips out a baking sheet dotted with tiny little pies. It's about ninety billion degrees in here, enough to make the Devil himself sweat, and Mama's hair is starting to frizz in spite of Lustrasilk.

"What are you baking?" I say.

She spares me a glance. "Raspberry tarts and strawberry chiffon pie." She sets the tarts on the counter. "Well, the chiffon pie is in the fridge already, and just needs a touch of whipped cream and generosity."

My mouth is watering something fierce, but I frown. "Generosity? What for?"

"For the luncheon, of course!"

The luncheon. I clean forgot. She's hard at work concocting dainties and delights for the Monroe County Society of Cookery, never mind that those snobby old ladies are only pretending to be dainty and delightful themselves.

"Oh," I say. "So by generosity, you mean the Society digs deeper in their wallets?"

Mama gives me a look. "You have half an hour to make

yourself look presentable."

I groan.

Daddy saunters into the kitchen, sleepy-eyed and smiling. "Is all this for breakfast?"

"No," Mama says. "And aren't you going to be late for work?"

"Not yet." Daddy keeps his eyes on Mama's, but he sneaks his hand behind his back and reaches for a glistening raspberry tart.

"Laurent!" Mama swats him with her spatula. "Those tarts are off-limits."

Daddy licks his finger. "Ah, but forbidden tarts taste so much sweeter." He leans in to give Mama a kiss, but she dodges him.

"The Society's coming," I warn him.

Mama turns on me. "Brush your hair, Josephine. Heavens, I let my children run wild."

I skulk out of there before she prods me to go faster. I don't have an excuse to escape this round of braiding my hair so tight it hurts, putting on my white sandals, and wearing a sundress Mama sewed for me. It's a pretty key-lime green, but the cut makes it look more girly than glamorous. Not like anything Authelia would wear.

When will the Devil's Own Dill Pickles start working? The cookbook didn't say. Maybe Shaula would tell me, if I could get in touch with her. Grimacing, I turn toward my bedroom mirror, but of course it's shattered and gone.

Downstairs, quick footsteps cross the floor, and then the front door protests with a squeal of rusty hinges. I hear muffled voices.

"Mrs. Silkie!" Mama says. "You're early, I was just serving the refreshments."

The witches have begun to arrive.

So now I'm doomed to stand by the front door, smile, nod, and take the ladies' jackets and hats. I have no idea why they bother wearing any at all, but they always come sweating in their Sunday best, trying to fluff their hair and powder their noses the instant they have a chance, no match for the Missouri heat.

"Josephine! So good to see you."

"Always nice to meet a young lady with such gracious manners."

"Miss DeLune, you are the spitting image of your mother."

The Society ladies look like eggs from the same dozen, with tidy little hats over hair in shades of white, gray, and salt-and-pepper. They all smell the same, too, like too-sweet perfume, mothballs, and baby powder.

Of all the covens Mama could have joined... well, this *was* the only one. Slim pickings.

Now wait a minute. I don't recognize her.

A new witch climbs out of a turquoise Buick, taking bite-size steps in her pencil skirt. She doesn't look much older than me. Her strawberry blonde hair swirls up in a simple knot, and she keeps blinking like she's been in the dark for too long.

"Josephine!" Mama calls from the backyard, in a help-or-else tone.

Sweat breaks out on my forehead. I hurry through the house to the backyard, nearly trip and die over the garden hose, then make it alive to the tables beneath the magnolia. The ladies settle in their chairs, cooing over the beautiful raspberry tarts Mama made. I glance at the strawberry blonde witch, but she doesn't meet my eyes.

"Iced tea?" Mama asks the Society ladies, with a meaningful glance at me.

I pick up the pitcher, and they start gossiping in earnest.

"Did you see the hors d'oeuvres Mrs. Chantecler served? Dreadful things, with olives."

"Now, I always swear by cheese crackers to settle down the children. Don't you think?"

"Oh, but the wedding cake for Molly's reception was the absolute *finest*. Just a touch of conjure to make the icing sparkle just so."

Just a touch of conjure. That's all these witches are ever going to cook up. That, and the most boring chitchat this side of the Mississippi. I almost laugh at the silliness of it all. While they're prattling on about crackers and cake, the Ravenous One runs wild. Heavens, these old relics would keel over at the sight of him!

Kitty-corner from me, the new witch squints in the sun and doodles on her napkin. Who *is* she? I've never seen her around Paris; she must have just moved to Monroe County. She looks like the exact opposite of me—yet another girl content to be decorative and sweet without taking up too much space or talking too loud.

Basically, a waste of brains, if girls like that ever had any to begin with.

Mrs. Bourbon, a regular old witch with a turkey-wattle neck, leans over to Mama. Since she's more than a little deaf, I hear her "whisper" loud and clear. "I'm afraid John just doesn't look at me the way he used to... I'd love one of those chocolate cakes. The *special* kind." She puts her wrinkly hand on Mama's and raises her eyebrows.

"Certainly," Mama says.

"You're such an angel, Clara." Mrs. Bourbon beams.

Soon enough, Mrs. Bourbon isn't the only so-called witch asking Mama for something.

"I have a small favor to ask. Do you still bake cookies for sleepwalkers?"

"For my luncheon, I would love some of that refreshing potato salad. You know, the kind that makes it feel like a breeze is blowing even when the humidity is one hundred percent and everybody else is sweating like pigs."

"I would be very obliged if you could help me with a particular birthday party..."

If I were a gambling girl, I would bet that we're going

to hear about this birthday party, and that luncheon, in the society section of the Paris Gazette, and every one of these witches is going to take all the culinary glory for herself.

"Tell me," Mrs. Bourbon says, "when is Josephine planning on joining the Society?"

How about never?

"Soon." Mama gives her the biggest, fakest smile, but Mrs. Bourbon eats it up.

"Oh, how lovely! It's been years since we've had a mother-daughter pair in our Society. Fifty-three, to be exact. I remember when…"

I sneak away before I get sucked in any deeper.

Might as well refill the lemonade pitcher. I push open the kitchen door and blink as I pass from the sunshine to sudden dimness. Lord, it's so muggy in here. I fling open the fridge and lean inside, basking in the glorious chilliness.

A hand settles on my arm, and I jump—it's the new witch.

"Oh, I'm sorry! I didn't mean to startle you." She has this funny breathless way of talking, like she's afraid of being interrupted. She gives me a sweet, empty smile and offers me her hand. "Miss Elmyra Stieber."

I shake her hand, distracted by her bubblegum-pink nail polish. "Josephine."

"So pleased to meet you," she says. "I'm new here, and

I don't know *any*body."

As she talks, she waves around a dainty plate with a raspberry tart on it. The tart teeters on the edge. I can't tear my eyes away.

"Are you lost, Miss Stieber?"

"Oh, call me Elmyra. I just popped in here to powder my nose, but I stumbled upon the kitchen on the way out. Aren't these Formica countertops wonderful?"

I shrug. "Wonderful how? They do what countertops do."

Elmyra shakes her head. "Aren't you witty!" She glances out the window at Mama. "That's your mother, isn't it?"

"The one and only."

She touches my shoulder. "Maybe you can help me."

My stomach flops like a fish on land. I doubt she stumbled in here by accident. More likely she's snooping around, looking for Mama's secret recipes. What if *she* is the witch cooking conjure for McArthur Mills?

I narrow my eyes. "What kind of *help*?"

A shadow crosses over Elmyra's otherwise sunny face. "Well, I—"

There's a knock on the front door.

"Let me get that," I say, smiling through gritted teeth. "Head on back to the luncheon. I'll have some more lemonade in no time."

"Will do!" Elmyra says, oh-so-perky.

I jog to the door and open it, then take a step back.

Mr. Glumphy stands there in sweat-yellowed pajamas, a cardboard box cradled in his arms. His greasy hair shadows his sunken eyes.

"Delivery," he mumbles.

"For Mama?" I ask, not sure what else to say.

He shakes his head, slowly, and his voice slips into a hissing whisper. "For *you*."

The Ravenous One.

I slam the door in his face, my heartbeat leaping in my chest like a scared rabbit.

I run through the kitchen and into the backyard, where Mama cuts slices of strawberry chiffon pie for the Society ladies while they fan themselves and laugh. My legs feel slow and clumsy, like I'm wading through a nightmare. I wave both of my hands at Mama, but she's not looking, and now it's too late.

Mr. Glumphy shambles into the backyard, swaying slightly. Sweat trickles down his forehead, and his eyes burn with the fire of the Ravenous One. He's not carrying the fake package anymore, and his arms reach for me.

"Josephine," he says, his voice a hoarse whisper.

The postmaster in his pajamas finally catches Mama's attention. "Mr. Glumphy!"

When the Ravenous One sees Mama, he gives her a rabid-dog grin. A sour taste rises in my mouth. I step in front of Mama, praying he won't hurt her. Around us, the

Society sit frozen with forks and cups halfway to their mouths.

There's a pause, like the second you know you're way up high and about to fall.

"Clara?" Mrs. Silkie says. "Is that the postmaster? Is he ill?"

The Ravenous One uses Mr. Glumphy's mouth for a terrible hacking laugh.

Understanding slides over Mama's face. She grips my shoulder and walks backwards through the luncheon, tugging me with her.

"Stay close, Josephine," she murmurs. "He's possessed by something powerful."

I open my mouth to tell her he's the Ravenous One, but the words get stuck somewhere in my throat and choke me.

"I've had enough!" Mrs. Bourbon shoves her chair back and stands. "I'm going home."

Mr. Glumphy's eyes roll back in his head, and he falls to his knees. A black swarm of dust flies from his mouth and darts up Mrs. Bourbon's nose. She coughs, blinks a few times, then tosses aside her purse and turns in my direction.

Behind her, Mr. Glumphy climbs to his feet and looses a wordless moan.

A scream tears from Mrs. Silkie's throat, and that sets off the rest of the Society ladies. They shriek and scramble out of the backyard, knocking tarts and teacups to the ground. Mama stands like a statue in the garden.

Mr. Glumphy staggers to the nearest table and begins gobbling tarts. "Mmm."

The Society witches keep squawking.

"Zombie! Zombie!"

"Get that filthy creature away from me!"

"Oh, lord, please protect us from this unholy beast..."

The Ravenous One marches forward inside Mrs. Bourbon. Mrs. Chantecler stumbles in his way, and he darts into her body, then the next, and the next, zigzagging through the old ladies like they're nothing but stepping stones.

"Mama?" I whirl around, but she's not by my side. "Mama!"

What if the Ravenous One tries to possess her next? Or *me*?

I high-tail it out of there, only to trip over Mr. Glumphy. He's crawling on his knees, eating great handfuls of strawberry chiffon pie. He looks up at me with glazed eyes, chewing with his mouth open, and makes a happy grunt.

Something inside me snaps, and I start giggling hysterically. I chuck a raspberry tart at the zombie, and he grabs it with greedy hands.

"Josephine!" Mama's voice slices through the screams and moans. "Watch out!"

ELEVEN

I look up in the nick of time. Black tentacles of dust slither through the air. I hold my breath hard, my heart hammering. A sour-milk, road-kill stink trickles into my nose, and my eyes start watering. I stagger back, dizzy.

With calm fury in her eyes, Mama marches right up to the Ravenous One. "Leave."

The dust pulls back, clumping into a shadow-cloud, and starts to darken. A thrill of dread shoots down my spine. I remember the black tangle of ink in my grimoire, a tangle with a mouthful of deadly sharp teeth.

"Be careful, Mama!" I shout.

Mama grabs a saltshaker from her pocket and shakes some big salt crystals into her hand. She flings a wide sweep of salt at the Ravenous One, and the voodoo spirit shudders back with a horrible scream like metal being bent in two. His black shadow-tentacles shrink into his tangled body. Mama pelts him with more salt, and the Ravenous One falls apart into ragged scraps of shadow that crawl away to hide in the dirt.

I stand frozen, afraid he's going to reach up through the grass and grab my ankles.

Mama marches right across the lawn and looks me in the eye. "Are you all right?"

"I—I think so." Besides how much I'm shaking all over, I feel okay. "I didn't know plain old salt works on voodoo spirits."

"That wasn't plain old salt," Mama says. "It came from the bottom of the Dead Sea."

"Oh." I swallow. "Are you sure it's gone?"

"It won't come back for the time being. Not until the rain washes away my conjure."

I don't know anything about salt or rain, so I keep my mouth shut.

Mama scans the backyard. "Lord, look at this mess!"

A grand total of five zombies shuffle around the ruined luncheon, pawing at cakes and licking frosting off their fingers. The rest of the Society ladies appear to have escaped in one piece. Mr. Glumphy is nowhere to be seen.

"What... what *was* it?" I say.

Mama fixes me with a long hard stare, and for a moment I'm scared she's going to see inside my soul and tug out the truth.

"Trouble far out of your league," she says.

I chew on the inside of my cheek. I can't ask any more questions, or she's going to know I've already been playing with Major League Trouble.

Mama grabs a plateful of pie, her back straight. "Let's get down to business."

***

I sit at the table with Daddy and Cleon, my head hunched over a plateful of fried catfish and lima beans that Mama threw together. Night lurks and lumps up against our windows, greedy for our light. I glance and glance again at the cracks between the curtains, scared I might see undead fingers sliding down the glass.

Cleon glances sideways at me, but Daddy touches his finger to his lips.

Mama's on the phone with *her* mama, my Grandma Lula, in the kitchen.

"No! I told you already—no, she didn't—yes, we locked them in the barn."

"Whoa." Cleon leans over and whispers in my ear. "You locked the zombies in the *barn*? You mean the *one in our backyard*?"

I nod and pop a piece of catfish into my mouth.

"Oh, wow." Cleon sounds gleeful. "The Ralstons are going to pee themselves!"

"Hush," Daddy says in a low voice. "Your mother

knows what she's doing."

"I hope so," I mutter.

Mama's talking loud enough we can't help but hear every word she says. "I double and triple-checked my conjure. Those zombies won't be getting out of that barn, and nobody's going to be getting in there, neither."

Daddy clears his throat. "Jo?" he whispers. "Are you certain the neighbors saw nothing?"

I shrug. "We lured them in there pretty quick. Zombies love cake."

Cleon's trying not to laugh, I can tell.

"Of course not!" Mama says to Grandma Lula. "She could never do a thing like that. It's obvious she doesn't have the knack for it."

Hot shame sweeps over my face. They can only be talking about *me*.

"Well, we'll see about that." Mama's voice quiets a little. "I guess so..."

I'm sure Grandma Lula's talking her ear off right now. They always have argued about my talent with conjure, or lack of it. A tingle stirs in my belly. What will Grandma Lula say to me when I tell her she was right all along?

"What did this spirit look like?" Daddy whispers, looking at me.

"Didn't Mama tell you?" I whisper back.

He purses his lips. "She was too upset."

"A big black squiggly thing like an octopus in a

tornado. With nasty teeth."

Cleon's eyebrows shoot up. "Really? Like an octopus? Did it sort of crawl, or…?"

Mama's shoes rap across the floor, and we fall silent. She's breathing a bit hard, like she was just running a mile instead of talking to Grandma Lula. Her hair frizzes out at crazy angles, and she tries to smooth it with her hands.

"Well! That's settled."

We all look at Mama, wondering what she means.

She sighs. "Grandma Lula's visiting a friend in Memphis right now, but she's convinced herself this is an emergency. She's driving up to Paris first thing, and she should be here some time later tonight or early next morning." Mama pantomimes slapping herself on the forehead. "Lord, the guest bedroom isn't ready!"

Daddy folds his napkin and stands. "I'll help."

"Grandma Lula!" Cleon grins at me. "This is going to be great."

"I wish I shared your enthusiasm," I mutter.

When Grandma Lula comes, it's going to be twice as hard pretending I haven't been playing with the recipes in her cookbook.

***

Midnight sneaks by, and I can't sleep.

I lie on my bed and watch the shadows of tree branches

sway on the ceiling. Shaula sits beside me, so light she doesn't even dent the mattress, and strokes my hair with her whisper-soft touch. There's a strange hollow craving in the pit of my stomach, a hunger for something that doesn't make much sense to me yet.

"I should have done something," I say, my voice husky. "I was damn near useless."

"You are here in one piece. That is enough for now."

I roll away from her touch. "But he turned five of those old ladies into zombies. And now they're locked in that barn out there, all by themselves... do zombies get afraid, Shaula? Do they know who they are right now?"

She shakes her head, her eyes glimmering full of dark secrets.

I blow out my breath. "What do I do now? How do I get good enough to stop him?"

Outside, there's the pop and crackle of gravel beneath tires. I run to my window and press my face to the cool windowpane.

A dusty old black Ford pulls into our driveway and flicks off its headlights.

"Grandma Lula!" I whisper.

I glance at Shaula, but she's already gone invisible again. Still in my nightie, I run downstairs and crash into Mama.

"Josephine!" She nearly jumps out of her skin. "Why aren't you in bed?"

"Grandma Lula's here," I say.

Sure enough, there's a knock on the door.

"Answer it," Mama says. "Wait, give me a minute to tidy the kitchen...!"

As my hand closes on the doorknob, I think of Mr. Glumphy standing outside with his sweaty pajamas and dull eyes, and my muscles seize up. The Ravenous One could be out there right now, possessing some unfortunate person.

But that's silly, I just saw Grandma Lula drive up! Lord, what's come over me?

I draw in a deep breath and fling open the door.

Grandma Lula tosses aside her bulging shopping bags and drags me into an anaconda-tight hug. Her orange blossom perfume clouds over me, and it's like I'm eight years old and I'm back in the shimmering heat of a Louisiana summer.

"Jo-Jo!" Grandma Lula says, her strong voice humming through me. "You've grown!"

"I'm not really Jo-Jo anymore," I say, blushing.

Grandma Lula draws back to get a proper look at me, and I do the same. She's decked out in pearls, a black turtleneck, and a tailored skirt, like she's still selling fine china at Macy's instead of getting ready to wrangle a zombie.

"Grandma Lula!" Mama says. "You're early."

"Of course I am," Grandma Lula says, not batting an

eye. "Sounds like you have a serious voodoo problem up here."

I marvel at how Grandma Lula looks so much like Mama, only *more*. More elegance, more experience, more conjure bottled up inside. I can almost smell the magic hovering around her, mingling with her signature citrus perfume.

"Bring those bags inside," Mama says, "and we'll get started."

I grab a fancy Macy's shopping bag. "I'll help."

As Grandma Lula lugs the rest of her bags through the doorway, Mama catches her and gives her a giant hug. The two of them laugh, and it's a soft wondering laugh, like they're both thinking, "What took so long?"

I carry the Macy's bag into the kitchen, and stop short in the doorway. All manner of bottles and jars are scattered across the Formica countertops. Sitting open on a stool, I glimpse a book bound in violet leather—Mama's grimoire. Words swim lazily across the pages, and I slide my feet closer, itching to take a peek.

"Josephine?" Mama says, suddenly behind me in the doorway.

I tear my gaze away from her grimoire and put on my best innocent face. "Yes?"

"Aren't you tired?" she says, in a tone that implies I definitely should be.

I square my shoulders. "I can't sleep. Not after what

happened today."

She blows her breath out through her nose. "I'm sorry, but I don't have time to help you with nightmares. I've got bigger fish to fry."

An awful silly image of a deep-fried zombie pops into my head.

I keep a straight face. "Can I come with you? To find the zombies?"

"Zombies?" Mama shakes her head. "You've had enough of those for one day."

Grandma Lula brushes past Mama, lugging more bags inside, and gives me a once over. "Clara, let her help. She's old enough."

Mama plants her hand on her hip. "I don't think—"

"I know what you think." Grandma Lula waves away her comment, then gives me a once over. "Jo-Jo, you'd better get dressed."

Behind her, Mama sighs and glances heavenward. "And wear sensible shoes!"

***

With Mama at the wheel of the Fireflite, we swoosh along the back roads to Paris.

I stare straight through the windshield, watching the yellow stripes on the road roll underneath us. Rain begins to clatter on the roof of the car, and the night darkens. I feel like we're in a submarine floating along the bottom of the ocean.

In the back, Grandma Lula rummages through a Macy's bag. "Here we are."

Mama glances sideways at her. "Are you serious?"

"Dead serious." Grandma Lula lifts out a casserole dish. "Black Magic Brownies."

I stretch forward and take a deep whiff. A gorgeous bittersweet smell creeps up into my nose and makes me drool. The brownies are dark like a black cat, and glossy in a way I just know is going to crunch when I bite into them.

"Did you put panther's tears in those?" Mama says.

Grandma Lula smiles. "The very *best* panther's tears."

"What for?" I say.

"Sharp eyes, of course." Grandma Lula hands me a brownie. "Try one."

Mama glances at me in the review mirror. "Hold on one second, Josephine!"

I freeze, the brownie halfway to my mouth.

"Are you sure you want her eating such powerful conjure?" Mama says to Grandma Lula. "I'm not sure she can stomach it."

I glower. "Sharp eyes don't sound too horrible."

Mama shakes her head. "Oh, believe me, that's not the only thing a Black Magic Brownie is going to do to you. Eat a Black Magic Brownie, and you won't be able to stop smelling all the dark conjure for miles around."

"And ain't that exactly what we need right now?" Grandma Lula says in a sassy voice.

"There could be *side effects*," Mama whispers.

The brownie's scent trickles into my mouth, teasing me with how close I am to tasting it. Good lord, it smells good. "Like what?"

Mama twists back to look at me. "Let's just say a lot of the ingredients in Black Magic Brownies are the same ones you'd bake into a batch of Misfortune Cookies. If something's a teensy bit off, that's bad luck for a week."

"Oh, for heaven's sake!" Grandma Lula says. "You think *my* recipe is—"

A deer soars from the bushes and bounds across the road.

"Watch out!" I scream.

Mama brakes swiftly, and we come to a lurching halt. "I see it."

Her voice sounds calm, but she clenches the steering wheel with white knuckles. The deer stands in the glow of our headlights, its eyes glowing green, its flanks shivering. Then the animal zigzags away into the trees.

Mama lifts her foot from the brake pedal. "Everybody okay?"

I nod, then realize I'm clenching the brownie in my fist. It's starting to crumble.

"You have enough bad luck without my brownies,"

Grandma Lula mutters.

Mama pretends not to hear, but I see her roll her eyes. "Well, we've stopped. Let's eat."

"Roll down the windows," Grandma Lula says. "Might be magic right under our noses."

With the windows down, the rush of rain hushes us. Right now all I can smell is wet asphalt and swamp. I stare at the brownie in my hand, then scoop it into my mouth. Deep dark chocolate bursts in my mouth, twisted up with a sharpness like lemon peel and lightning in the air. I shut my eyes and swallow.

"Delicious," I moan. "Can I have another one?"

"One is enough," Mama says sternly. She nibbles her Black Magic Brownie delicately, as if she's afraid it might bite back.

Grandma Lula devours her Black Magic Brownie in three bites. "*Délicieux.*"

She sounds *so* much like Shaula. The brownie crumbs stick to the roof of my dry mouth. Should I tell them the truth?

"There we go," Mama whispers. She tilts her head back and sniffs the air.

I clear my throat. "What does black magic smell like, anyway...?"

A scent creeps into my nose and lingers in the back of my throat. A dark, dark scent like sour plum skins and the perfume of rain at midnight in a moonless sky. Then the wind blows the other way, and the scent vanishes.

"It's coming from the east," Grandma Lula says.

Mama nods and starts to drive. We cruise through the forest, then take a right at the nearest stop sign. The dark conjure smell gusts into the convertible, and Mama pulls over by the crooked sign for the town dump.

A man stands at the top of the hill, his back to us, his clothes drenched with rain. He crouches, grabbing something from the trash and shoving it into his mouth like a clumsy baby. Bits fall to the ground as he chews.

I shiver and hug myself, goosebumps dotting my arms. "Is it coming from the dump?"

"I don't think so," Mama says, "but pretty close to it."

I open my mouth to reply, then hiccup so hard it startles me.

"Hiccups?" Grandma Lula says.

I frown, then hiccup again. "From the brownie?"

Mama sighs. "Be glad it's not worse bad luck." She unbuckles her seatbelt. "Follow me."

I jump out of the Fireflite. Grandma Lula pops open a black umbrella, even though the rain's nothing more than a drizzle now. Mama points her nose into the wind and stalks into the darkness. It's more swamp than forest here, squishy underfoot, with clusters of skunk cabbages out-stinking the smell of dark conjure.

In the murky shadows, there's a moan.

I stop dead in my tracks, but Mama and Grandma Lula

don't seem to notice. They pick their way through the mud and mushy grass. My heartbeat thumps against my ribs, and a hiccup lurches from my throat.

There's another moan, louder. It sounds like it's coming from the bushes.

"Mama?" I say, my voice wavering. "Grandma Lula?"

The two of them stop and glance back, irritation plain on their faces.

"Did you—" I hiccup. "—hear that?"

Grandma Lula shakes raindrops from her umbrella. "Child, I just hear your hiccups."

"No!" I shake my head fiercely. "Over there."

I force my legs to move, dragging me closer to the bushes. I hold my breath tight, fighting my hiccups, but one breaks free anyway.

A growling moan rumbles close by my ear.

I whirl around, shaking, and look straight into the cloudy eyes of a zombie.

TWELVE

The zombie reaches for me with clumsy arms. His skin looks like a drowned earthworm. His wet hair plasters his forehead, and mud streaks his mouth. No, not mud—chocolate. He's been eating rotten cake from the dump.

It's Horton.

"Sweet Jesus," Grandma Lula whispers. "This is worse than I thought."

"His neck," Mama says. "Look at his neck."

A twist of blackberry bramble circles his neck like a spiked dog collar. It looks too tight, digging into his skin. More blackberry brambles circle his wrists like painful bracelets. I'm not sure the zombie even feels them. I hope not.

"Binding conjure." Grandma Lula grimaces. "Strong, dark conjure."

Mama sniffs the air. "This is it. The conjure. But the

wrong zombie!"

Horton swallows, and the brambles scratch his Adam's apple. "Cake?"

The poor zombie sounds so hopeful. His eyes burn with a peculiar craving for conjure.

"A voodoo spirit did this," Grandma Lula says. "No, more than one spirit. One of them much older than the other."

Shaula and the Ravenous One.

"One is the spirit that attacked us at the luncheon," Mama says. "I'm sure of it."

"And the other?" Grandma Lula says.

"I don't know."

But I do.

Horton frowns, moving his mouth soundlessly like he's chewing on air.

Grandma Lula peers at him. "You're saying this is the wrong zombie?"

"Yes," Mama says.

"Then where's the right one?"

Mama shakes her head. "I don't know, but we'd better find out fast."

She takes a saltshaker from her purse and starts walking in a circle around Horton. The zombie watches her but makes no move.

"Be careful, Mama!" I say.

Grandma Lula lays her hand on my shoulder. "The

zombie can't walk. Not now."

Tears prick my eyes. "Horton. His name was Horton."

Mama sprinkles a thick circle of Dead Sea salt around the zombie. He paws at her but misses, his fingers swiping the air.

Horton's mouth twists into a grimace. "No cake."

I blink fast. This is my fault. If I hadn't gone looking for my grimoire in the dump, Horton would never be undead.

"We need to help him," I say.

Grandma Lula thins her lips, her fingers tightening on my shoulder. "We can't."

"But—there's a countercurse." I realize what I'm saying as I say it. "Isn't there?"

Grandma Lula stares into my eyes for a long moment. "What makes you say that?"

The bottom of my stomach drops out. Shaula lied to me.

"They're going to be zombies forever?" I say. "Horton and Mr. Glumphy and all the ladies from the Society of Cookery are... dead?"

Mama starts a second circle of salt around the zombie. "Not yet."

I stare into Grandma Lula's eyes, searching for answers.

She stares right back at me. "There might be a way, but it's at the bottom of a swamp."

Which swamp? The one in Louisiana I'm never going to forget...?

"We need to move." Mama marches toward the road. "Come on."

We leave the zombie trapped in a ring of salt, and squish through the swamp as fast as we can. I trail behind Mama and Grandma Lula, because I can't help glancing back at Horton. He stands there with slumped shoulders, his head drooping, like a doll nobody's playing with anymore. I wish I had some cake to give him.

"*Josephine.*"

A whisper on the wind. Not Mama, not Grandma Lula. Rain drips from the clouds and plops on my skin, trickling with my sweat.

"Josephine."

The voice is stronger now, nearer.

I freeze, my legs shaking. The shadows of tree branches claw at me, and the raindrops feel cold on my skin.

"Who is it?" I whisper, my voice shriveling in my throat.

"You know who I am."

The rain. Mama said salt would stop the Ravenous One until the rain came, and washed away her conjure. I turn in a slow circle, looking around the swamp, but the Ravenous One might as well be invisible in this thick darkness.

"Josephine!" Grandma Lula hollers from the road. "Now's not the time for sightseeing."

Her voice breaks the paralysis of my legs, and I sprint

for the Fireflite. The skin on the back of my neck prickles, and I try to hold my breath, my lungs burning, so the Ravenous One can't creep into me through my mouth.

I dart into the Fireflite and slam the door.

Mama sits behind the wheel, as cool as a cucumber. "Ready?"

I nod, since I don't trust my voice.

Mama guns the engine, the needle on the speedometer passing numbers that would make Daddy cringe. The rain rushes into a downpour like giant hands wringing out a dishcloth above our heads. Water hisses under the tires, spraying into overflowing ditches, and the windshield wipers *swish-thump, swish-thump.*

"Lord, we won't smell any dark conjure now," Grandma Lula says.

Mama purses her lips. "Not after the rain washes the scent away."

We cruise slowly into town and wind along every street in Paris like we're lost in a labyrinth. I keep my eyes peeled for zombies. The rain finally peters out, and the fresh-scrubbed face of the moon peeks out from the clouds.

"Let's get some sleep," Mama says, "and keep looking in the morning."

I blow out my breath, but I'm not sure I can afford to be relieved.

Back at home, I climb upstairs to my bedroom on aching legs. I shuck off my wet clothes, tug on my cozy nightie, and plunge into bed.

A clatter of gravel hits my window.

"Quentin?"

My heartbeat leaps like a grasshopper. I grab my dressing gown and tug it over my nightie, then hurry over to the window.

Far down below, small and pale in the moonlight, stands a girl. She's wearing a *hat*. In the middle of the night. Who's that kind of crazy? A zombie? My stomach clenches, and I taste bitterness creeping over my tongue.

I slide open the window. "Who is it?"

The girl looks up at me, and I gasp. Authelia.

"Josephine?" she says.

I swallow hard, and my tongue sticks to the roof of my dry mouth. "What do you want?"

"Get down here." Her voice sounds wobbly. "I don't know what to do."

This could be a trick. But I bite the inside of my cheek, and nod.

Slipping my shoes over my bare feet, I creep out the back door. Authelia waits for me beneath the moonshadows of the magnolia tree. She keeps her head bowed beneath her wide-brimmed hat. I drag my feet closer to her, afraid to look.

"Look at me," Authelia whispers, and she tosses her hat from her head.

A gasp escapes before I can help myself, and I clap my hands to my mouth.

This isn't the Authelia I remember. Her golden locks are gone, replaced by a stinking heap of wet green hair, like somebody scooped up a handful of moss and swamp weeds and dumped it on her head. Foul-smelling water drips down her forehead and cheeks, and she swats at a cloud of gnats that buzzes around her stench.

This is my ugly, ugly revenge.

"I don't know what's wrong with me," Authelia says, and it's as if all the luster has gone from her voice. "It started this evening. I've been hiding in my bedroom this whole night because my hair keeps getting worse and worse."

I suck in a slow, shaky breath. "Why did you come to me?"

"Did your mother do this to me?" There's a hungry desperation in her eyes. "Why? I mean, I know she's a witch, but—"

I shush her and glance back at my house. "Keep it down!"

"But I don't know why *me*. I'm one of her customers. I *paid* her for a pie!"

The Sweetheart Pie. Like I could forget.

"No." I keep shaking my head. "It wasn't her."

"It has to be her!" Authelia's starting to sound hysterical. "Who else would—?"

A light flicks on inside, flooding the backyard with light. Authelia gasps and snatches up her silly hat. She darts into the bushes like a startled deer, and I leap around the corner of the house, shrinking against the scratchy wood.

"Who's out there?" Mama shouts into the night.

I peek around the corner and see her standing in the kitchen doorway, silhouetted in all her dressing gown glory. Her gaze latches onto me.

"Mama!"

We stare at each other.

"Josephine Elle DeLune," she says in a velvety, dangerous voice, "you'd better have an excellent reason why you're sneaking out at night."

"I'm not sneaking *out*," I say, "I'm going back *in*."

Mama does not look amused. "Get yourself in here before I—"

Behind me, the bustles rustle and shake. All the muscles in my legs tighten up, and I couldn't run even if I wanted to.

"Mrs. DeLune?" Authelia whispers.

She steps into the light, her hat clenched in both hands, and looks up at us.

Mama sucks in her breath with a hiss. "Authelia

McArthur? Is that you?"

Authelia nods, tears glimmering in her eyes, and I feel my own eyes sting.

"Honey, what happened to your *hair*?" Mama says.

"Don't tell me you don't know," Authelia says in a horrified tone.

I clench my hands into fists, my fingernails digging into my palms, then take a step forward. "It was me. I fed her some conjure."

"You did?" Mama and Authelia say at the same time.

"Yes."

Mama clenches her jaw, her nostrils flaring. "Get inside," she murmurs. "Both of you."

I can tell Mama's a split second away from losing her temper.

I nod and scramble through the door, my heartbeat pounding. Authelia follows close at my heels, and then we're both standing together in the kitchen. Her hair looks even more disgusting in the light, and I try not to stare.

"Don't budge an inch," Mama says, like we'd dare think otherwise, and she marches off.

"Why did you do it?" Authelia says in a tiny voice.

My face feels hot, then cold. "Why do you think?"

She stares at the linoleum.

I count specks in the Formica countertops for an eternity or two until, finally, Mama comes back with Grandma Lula alongside. Grandma Lula looks quite the spectacle in pajamas of shimmering purple silk embroidered with dragons.

"Lord!" Grandma Lula says, staring at Authelia's hair. "That *is* a nasty curse."

Authelia cringes, and I feel pretty nasty myself.

"Sit," Mama says, like we're dogs.

Me and Authelia pick chairs at opposite ends of the kitchen table. This feels an awful lot like a trial, or maybe an interrogation.

Mama fills a kettle with water and sets it on the stove. "What kind of tea do you fancy?"

"Peppermint?" I say croakily.

Mama fixes her stare on Authelia. "You?"

"Peppermint sounds good," she whispers, flicking away a gnat.

While Mama fixes us some tea—hopefully conjure-free tea—Grandma Lula sits opposite us at the table and steeples her fingers.

"Well now," Grandma Lula says. "Time for you to tell us the truth."

I sink lower in my seat. "I haven't been lying."

Grandma Lula looks sideways at me. "You haven't been telling me the whole truth, either. I knew it the moment I set foot in Missouri."

Uh-oh.

I gulp a deep breath. "Grandma Lula, I know I shouldn't have been playing with the recipes in your cookbook, but I honestly didn't think the Devil's Own Dill Pickles were going to turn out so horrible. I wouldn't have given them to Authelia otherwise, but I wanted to get better at conjure. It wasn't my idea, it was Shaula's—"

"Shaula!" A teacup falls from Mama's hand and shatters on the floor. "You talked to that—that voodoo spirit?"

Authelia sits petrified in her chair, unblinking, and even the gnats in her hair quiet.

"Shaula came to me," I say. "I first saw her in the swamp." With a phantom of a drowned Authelia, but of course I don't say that out loud.

"Good lord, Josephine!" Mama says. "And you didn't think to tell me? Why—"

Grandma Lula silences her with a look. "What did Shaula want from you?"

"Shaula wanted to help me." I sit up a bit straighter. "She said she could teach me how to control my conjure, and to be a better witch."

Mama scoffs. "Shaula only helps herself."

"No!" My ears burn. "You've got it all wrong. Shaula has been watching over us."

"You think she's some guardian angel?" Mama bites off her words. "She was a black mark on our family tree."

I suck in my breath. "So she *is* my great-great-grandma?"

"Was," Grandma Lula says. "Up until the moment she became a voodoo spirit."

I nod hard. "She said the Ravenous One tried to eat her soul. Now he's after mine."

Grandma Lula looks straight into my eyes. "The Ravenous One?" she says, oh-so-softly.

I sink down even lower in my seat. "I saw him in the flames—there was a grease fire at Daddy's restaurant. He looked like a monster made out of fire, and he disappeared when I sprayed him with the fire extinguisher. But he came for me again at the dump, and I didn't think I was going to get away, but Shaula tricked him. That's when he turned Horton into a zombie. You already know about the zombies at the luncheon."

"I see," Grandma Lula says, her face unreadable.

Mama stands with her hand pressed to her mouth. The kettle starts whistling. She flicks off the stove and starts serving tea on autopilot.

"Zombies?" Authelia says, her face ghostly. "Zombies, here in Paris?"

"I'm afraid so," Mama says. "Drink your tea before you faint!"

Authelia slurps the tea and winces when she scalds her mouth, but at least some color returns to her cheeks. "What's the Ravenous One?"

"Something you should hope never to see, child," Grandma Lula says.

Gee, that makes me feel so much better.

I smooth my curls back from my face. "Have you seen

him before?"

"No. And not Shaula for..." Grandma Lula squints and tilts her head up. "Twenty years, if I recollect correctly. It was a potluck down in Louisiana. Some witch had got her conjure mixed up, and everybody who ate her Butterscotch Pie started seeing spirits. Shaula floated into a windowpane, looked at me, and floated on by."

"So you didn't talk to her," I say.

"Heavens, why would I want to do that?" Grandma Lula arches her eyebrows. "Shaula played with some dark, dark conjure in her time. It's no wonder she spirited herself away after the Ravenous One came looking for her."

"Well, if she's bad, so am I. Seeing as how the Ravenous One keeps calling my name."

Authelia gulps her tea. "You all must be busy." She pushes her chair from the table. "I'd better get going, it's so late—"

"Sit back down," Grandma Lula says. "We're not done with you."

"But I'm not even supposed to know all this!" Authelia wails. "Voodoo and zombies?"

"Too late. You're staying here until Josephine cooks up a countercurse for those pickles. Shouldn't take more than an hour or so."

"A countercurse?" I say. "But I don't know how to—"

"Shush," Grandma Lula says. "Clara? Break out the

cookbooks."

Mama nods. "I have just the recipe in mind..."

I sink so low in my chair that I almost side out the bottom. There's no getting out of this one, not after they got the truth out of me. Mama flips through *The New American Conjure Cookbook*, then slaps it in front of me.

"That one," she says, her finger on a page.

I lean forward and read the recipe.

MRS. BEULAH MAYBERRY'S AMELIORATING BUTTERMILK BISCUITS

Works even on tough hexes. Use extra buttermilk for an especially smooth countercurse, and go easy on the salt. Best served with Revitalizing Raspberry Jam.

"Ameliorating?" I say. "What's that?"

"It means making something better," Grandma Lula says. "Like you need to do now."

Mama leans over my shoulder and reads the list of ingredients out loud. "Buttermilk, flour, baking powder, juniper, angelica... I'm clean out of buttermilk. We're going to the Higgledy-Piggledy, and then you're going to get started."

***

In the Higgledy-Piggledy parking lot, the four of us

clamber out of the Fireflite. My legs feel like noodles, and it's not just from sitting so close to Authelia in the car. How am I going to bake these Ameliorating Buttermilk Biscuits without making an even bigger mess of things? I've never cooked light conjure, no thanks to Shaula.

Grandma Lula strides through the sliding doors of the Higgledy-Piggledy, her pumps clacking on the linoleum. Me and Mama follow hot on her heels. Authelia trails a little way behind us, flinching at the fluorescent lights, and I can see why—her hair is getting uglier by the second as the Devil's Own Dill Pickles take hold. I half-expect to see a salamander slithering out of the mossy tangle of hair over her left ear.

"Buttermilk should be in the back," Mama says.

But I'm distracted by the floor. Muddy footprints lead from the doors to the frozen aisle.

"I have a bad feeling about this," I mutter.

I follow the footprints and peek down the frozen aisle.

Authelia gasps. "Oh. My. God."

Mr. Glumphy sits on the floor with his feet out front, looking all the world like a giant baby. He holds a freezer open, pawing at boxes of McArthur Mills cheesecake. A cheesecake tumbles into his lap, strawberries askew. The zombie digs his dirty fingernails into the cake, digs out a sloppy handful, and smashes it into his mouth.

Mr. Glumphy smiles. "Good!"

"This must be the zombie we're looking for," Grandma

Lula deadpans.

"The cheesecake," I whisper. "Of course."

"Of course what?" Mama says.

Curse her and her sharp hearing.

I don't beat around the bush. "You remember that new witch at the luncheon? Elmyra Stieber? She's been snooping around your kitchen, trying to steal your recipes. And I sure as heck think she's working for McArthur Mills."

Mama's mouth thins into a line. "Figures."

Then it dawns on me, and I slap my forehead.

"Elmyra Stieber *is* Riley E. Bates," I say.

"Bates?" Mama says. "The author of 'Beware of Baked Black Magic'?"

"Think about it. Their names share all the same letters, only jumbled around. Riley E. Bates must be Elmyra Stieber's pen name. I'll bet my biscuits that witch wrote for the newspaper to make our cooking look bad."

I glance at Authelia to see her reaction, but she's too busy staring at the zombie.

Mr. Glumphy slaps the ruined cheesecake aside and starts chewing on another box. He rips it open with his teeth, so hard that a blueberry flies out and hits Authelia's pretty little shoe. She shrieks and dances back.

"Cake!" Mr. Glumphy says brightly, slapping both hands into the cheesecake mess.

"I have something better than cake." Grandma Lula

rummages in a shopping bag and pulls out a cinnamon roll. "Come and get it."

I can practically taste the conjure wafting from the cinnamon roll. The zombie sure can.

"Mmm?" Mr. Glumphy staggers to his feet.

Authelia shrieks again. "Keep it away from me!"

"Oh, honestly, don't be a wimp," I say.

"Girls!" Mama says. "That's enough."

Authelia's pale cheeks flush. "You can't—"

The lights above us buzz, then blink out.

Darkness.

I hear scattered shouts and gasps all around the Higgledy-Piggledy, and Mr. Glumphy's bare feet slap on the floor nearby.

"Turn on the lights," Authelia whimpers. "Please turn on the—"

"Hush!" Grandma Lula draws closer to me. I can feel the warmth of her body on mine. "There's a terrible darkness here."

"All I can see is darkness," I say, my voice wobbling.

Mama rummages in her purse and pulls out a flashlight. It's a teeny-tiny flashlight, with a little wimpy beam of light. She points it at Authelia, who's crying, and then at Mr. Glumphy, who's frowning and staring down the aisle.

"Why isn't he interested in cake anymore?" I whisper. "Or cinnamon rolls?"

Grandma Lula slips her hand over my mouth. "Don't

breathe a word."

A deathly silence presses against my ears. Mama shines her flashlight in a circle, the beam glinting off the freezers and casting crazy reflections. I see myself standing there, with Grandma Lula at my side, and Shaula behind us.

Shaula! Her outline gleams in the glass. Can nobody else see her?

I grab Grandma Lula's hand to pry it from my mouth, but Shaula shakes her head and mouths one soundless word. I can't read her lips because Mama keeps moving the flashlight and Shaula's too dim in the shadows.

She mouths the word again.

Run.

I yank Grandma Lula's hand from my mouth. "Run!"

THIRTEEN

Pandemonium. Authelia's screams block out Mama's shouting in my ear. I latch onto Grandma Lula's arm and start dragging her as I run, away from the terrible darkness coming nearer, coming to life.

"*Josephine.*"

The hiss crawls into my ear and rattles around my brain.

"*Josephine.*"

I chance a glance back and see black tentacles writhing against the ceiling and the floor. All the glass in all the freezers shatters at once. It falls in a glittering rain. Time seems to have slowed to a molasses crawl, black and thick and impossible to wade through. Authelia leaps for me and clutches my hand as if I'm the one who can save her.

"*You belong to me.*"

The Ravenous One must be so close. I can feel his

breath on my neck. Or maybe that's Authelia, terrified, clinging to me like I have a clue.

Mama stands in the middle of everything, staring straight at the tentacles and teeth.

"Run!" I yell. "It's the Ravenous One!"

"I know," Mama says.

The Ravenous One looms over her, a tangle of monstrous shadows. He opens his mouth and bares ring upon ring of fangs.

He wants me. He wants me, not Mama.

I lunge toward them, but Grandma Lula grabs my arm and anchors me down. I twist and try to break free, but she's too strong. The Ravenous One sighs, black smoke billowing from his mouth. Mama holds her ground.

No.

The Ravenous One bends over, slowly, and embraces Mama. She tilts her head up to look into the darkness, then takes a slow breath. The Ravenous One flows into her mouth, crawling into her body, possessing her.

No!

Mama doubles over and falls to her knees. I hear someone screaming, then realize it's me. I break free from Grandma Lula at last and run to Mama's side. She's swaying back and forth, her head bent, her face hidden.

My fingers shaking, I touch her shoulder. "Mama?"

She coughs, a horrible hard cough, then spits up a mouthful of salt. The Ravenous One rises back out of her mouth with a wildcat shriek. He floats above us, a tight ball of tentacles, then rips apart into ragged shadows and vanishes.

Above us, the lights flicker and buzz back on. My heartbeat still races against my ribs.

"He's gone," Grandma Lula says.

Mama slumps against a freezer, her skin sweaty, her eyes faraway.

I fall to my knees beside her. "Mama?" I rasp, my throat raw. "Can you hear me?"

"Salt," Grandma Lula says. "The Ravenous One won't fall for that trick twice."

There's a whimper behind me. Authelia's still here, crying.

"He's gone now," I say. "You're safe. Probably."

"Josephine," Authelia says, and her voice breaks on my name. "I'm so sorry."

A fierce ache swells in my throat. "It's too late for that."

She looks away, sobbing like it's her mother slumped on the floor. The burning behind my eyes escapes as hot tears.

"Is she... is she like Mr. Glumphy?" I swallow hard. "A zombie?"

"No," Grandma Lula says. "She's fighting the hunger. If we work hard, we can save her."

I squeeze Mama's hand. "You hear that? We're going to

save you. So hold on."

She gives my hand a tiny squeeze in reply.

***

Mama lies beneath a blanket, lost in a deep slumber. By the warmth of the lamplight, she nearly looks cozy, but I can't fool myself. Daddy sits at her bedside, holding her hand. He keeps rubbing her knuckles with his thumb.

"Help me give her a drink," Grandma Lula tells me.

She's carrying a teacup of lemongrass tea. The tangy scent prickles my nose. I prop another pillow under Mama's head, and Grandma Lula tilts the teacup at Mama's lips. Mama swallows out of reflex, her eyes still closed.

"Will that wake her?" Daddy says, his voice hoarse.

Grandma Lula shakes her head. "It's going to help her fight."

Mama doesn't look like she's fighting. She looks like she's slipping away into a sleep where none of us can touch her.

I kneel beside her and lay my head on her pillow. "Mama," I whisper. "Wake up soon."

I can smell the Lustrasilk in her hair, and my eyes get blurry with tears.

"Josephine." Grandma Lula squeezes my shoulder. "Let's give your mama some rest and head down to the kitchen, okay?"

I nod, wipe my cheeks dry, and kiss Mama on the forehead before I go.

***

Sun peeks through the kitchen windows, then invites itself inside, filling the room with a golden glow. I stand at the counter, my arms covered with flour up to my elbows, and knead a bowl of buttermilk biscuit dough.

"Careful," Grandma Lula says. "Knead it too much and it'll be tougher than leather."

I nod and keep my mind focused on the idea of amelioration, of making things better. Authelia perches on a stool near me, her eyes huge, since I'd bet she's never seen a witch cook any sort of conjure before. When the sunlight falls upon her face, her green hair almost looks pleasantly mossy—if you squint.

"I suspect that's kneaded enough," I say. "Time for the juniper and angelica."

The juniper comes in a mason jar, black berries and snakeskin leaves. I sprinkle a pinch into the biscuit dough, and the evergreen spice tingles in my nose. Every summer, Mama makes homemade candied angelica, thick stems like rhubarb sparkling with sugar crystals. I crunch a slice of angelica between my teeth and savor the herby licorice sweetness. The taste reminds me of Mama, and I have to take a steadying breath.

It's hard not to remember her blank face as she sleeps upstairs.

"So if I put some juniper and angelica in biscuits," Authelia says, "could I cure myself?"

"Don't be silly," Grandma Lula says. "That's not where conjure comes from."

Authelia blinks her big eyes. "Where *does* it come from?"

"Witches."

"Oh. Okay."

I take a tiny amount of pleasure in realizing that Authelia is indeed envious of me.

Grandma Lula folds her arms over her bosom. "For every teaspoon of talent, it takes a tablespoon of hard work. As my late husband was fond of saying. Of course, he couldn't do a lick of conjure, being a man, but he was right."

I try not to let her talking distract me, and count out thirteen slices of angelica for the biscuit dough. Thirteen because it's a lucky number for witches, as everybody knows. I dust off stray sugar crystals from my hands, then grab Mama's marble rolling pin and flatten the dough in smooth hard strokes, always from the center out.

"It *looks* good so far," Authelia says.

"Thanks," I say, "I guess."

Grandma Lula catches my eye. "Now, do you have any

particular shapes in mind?"

"Shapes...?" I lean over *The New American Conjure Cookbook*. "It doesn't say anything about shapes in here."

"Heavens, child, did you never watch your mama in the kitchen?"

A blush scalds my cheeks. "She never thought I was good enough to help, not for real."

"Don't you worry, Josephine." Grandma Lula purses her lips and pats me on the arm. "I can give you some pointers."

She yanks open a few drawers until she finds copper cookie cutters—hearts, clovers, flowers, butterflies, diamonds, and more. I let my gaze slide over the assortment of shapes, and it keeps coming back to the hearts.

"How about the hearts?" I say.

Grandma Lula nods and hands me the cookie cutter. "Hearts represent love and life. I don't know what Mrs. Beulah Mayberry had in mind for her buttermilk biscuits, but that shape should work just fine for curing a curse."

I puff up a little with pride, then set to work cutting the heart-shaped biscuits. When I'm done, Grandma Lula opens the oven door for me, and I slide the sheet inside. I set the timer for thirteen minutes, then dust off my hands.

Grandma Lula squeezes my shoulder. "I knew you had a knack for cooking."

"Thanks," I say.

She humphs. "I'm withholding final judgment until those biscuits come out of the oven."

I try to smile, but my mind wanders back to Mama. I haven't seen her for a little while. Daddy sat up with her until morning, when Grandma Lula told him he'd be more useful if he stopped pining and started driving to work.

"I'll check up on Clara," Grandma Lula says, like she's reading my mind.

I sigh and start washing my hands in the sink. Outside the kitchen window, I see Cleon pushing the lawnmower in a fury. He's trying to burn off his worries about Mama, but I'm not sure it's working. By the time he's done, there will be bare patches of dirt in our backyard. He stops to wipe sweat from his brow, then stares at the sky.

"Your brother looks pretty unhappy," Authelia says, behind me.

"Well," I say, "I'm not too happy either."

She sidesteps so I can grab the dishtowel and dry my hands. "I truly am sorry."

I keep my eyes locked on the sink. "About?"

"Everything."

I glance at her. "I'm sorry about cursing you. I know you don't believe me, but I didn't mean to pick such an awful recipe. Grandma Lula's cookbook is full of some nasty dark conjure, and I didn't know any better."

"I didn't deserve it," she says, with a hint of her old haughtiness. "Not entirely."

"But a little," I say. "Just a little."

She twists her lips and looks away. "Well, I got a nasty curse because I was being nasty. I'm not stupid. I know you hate my friends now, and they don't like you much, either. They think it's funny that I even talk to you."

I grit my teeth. "Funny? Not for me."

"I know that," she says. "But I wanted to make them laugh, you know? They're not all that bad, once you get to know them."

"Oh." I lean against the counter and cross my arms. "So they're better than me."

"No!" Authelia takes a ragged breath. "I just don't know how I can keep being friends with them and go back to being friends with you."

"From where I'm standing, it looks like you already made your choice."

Authelia shakes her head. "I don't want to be enemies anymore."

"Not if I'll curse you," I mutter.

She rolls her eyes and sighs dramatically. "You know what I mean! I'm sorry, okay?"

But I'm still not feeling inclined to accept her apology.

"Why did you buy Quentin a Sweetheart Pie?" I say.

Authelia shrugs airily. "All the popular girls have boyfriends. All of them except me. Quentin's clearly the cutest candidate for a boyfriend, but I found out the hard way he's the dumbest when it comes to flirtation."

"So you weren't trying to steal Quentin away?" I say.

Authelia stares at me. "What, from you?"

A blush burns my face, and I don't speak for fear of stammering.

"Josephine," Authelia says, "you can have him. The Sweetheart Pie didn't even work. I'm done playing around with magic."

I glance sideways at her. "Maybe we've both learned our lesson. But we'll see."

The oven buzzes, and I slide out the buttermilk biscuits. They're puffy little golden hearts, and they smell like spices from heaven.

I hand one, still hot, to Authelia. "Try it."

She takes a deep breath, then bites the biscuit. Curlicues of steam waft into the air. She closes her eyes and swallows hard. One second passes. Two. Three. Starting at her scalp, the green bleeds out of her hair and leaves behind blonde. The tangles and the stink vanish, and each one of the gnats disappears with a twinkle.

Authelia's eyes pop open. "Did it work?" She grabs a hunk of her hair and squeals.

"Don't bust my eardrums," I say.

Authelia lunges for me, and I flinch, but she drags me into a hug. I stand as stiff as a floorboard, then awkwardly hug her back.

She withdraws, her face pink. "Now we're even."

"I suppose," I say, and I bite back a smile.

Grandma Lula comes downstairs and claps me on the shoulder. "Glad to see those buttermilk biscuits did the trick."

Authelia twirls so that her hair fans out, and I feel only the tiniest pinch of envy.

"Your mama is resting," Grandma Lula says to me. "Not a zombie. Not yet."

A tiny speck of hope tingles in me. "How do we save her?"

"To undo the undead," Grandma Lula says, "you have to take away a zombie's hunger. And that means beating Hunger himself."

"We have to fight The Ravenous One?" I say.

"And win."

I swallow hard. That's a tall order, if I've ever heard one.

Grandma Lula drops her enormous purse onto the kitchen table with a thud, then takes a seat rather more gracefully. "I'm going to show you a secret. It's something I've had for years, but never had the occasion to use."

Me and Authelia share a glance, and then we each pull up a chair. Grandma Lula opens her purse ceremoniously and reaches inside.

There's a rap on the front door.

"Now, who's visiting this early?" Grandma Lula lumbers to her feet.

I follow her to the door, my heart pattering.

It's none other than Quentin Cole, with his greyhound and a bouquet of wilting dandelions. Flash wriggles past Quentin and starts licking my hand, though it's less frantic than it was right after he ate the Forget-Me-Not Pie.

Quentin looks taken aback to see Grandma Lula. "Good morning," he says, "Mrs...."

"Mrs. Bellerose," Grandma Lula says, leaning in the doorway, "but you can call me Grandma Lula like most everybody else."

When Quentin sees me, he blushes amazingly red. "Oh, is this your grandma?"

I nod and scratch Flash behind his ears.

"Josephine has told me lots about you, Mrs. Belle— Grandma Lula," he stammers. "All excellent things of course!"

"Of course," Grandma Lula says, with a knowing glance at me.

He holds out the dandelions. "These are for Josephine."

"Thank you," I say, and now I'm sure I'm blushing amazingly red.

"Why don't you come inside?" Grandma Lula says. "You look like you're about as wilted as those flowers. Going to get even hotter today."

"Thank you, ma'am," Quentin says.

I wince as we all walk back inside, thinking of Authelia, but she gives Quentin a cool once over and a polite, "Good morning."

Quentin just looks confused. Flash curls up under the kitchen table like he lives here.

Grandma Lula takes her purse. "Let me get this out of the way."

"Oh," I say, "Quentin's safe, Grandma Lula. He already knows we're witches. And... I may I have fed him some conjure, too."

Grandma Lula's eyebrows shoot skyward. "Did you now?"

I try not to look too sheepish. "A Forget-Me-Not Pie. But I think it's better now?"

Quentin nods vigorously. "I feel fine! Those flowers don't mean anything. I mean, they *do*, but..." His voice fades into a mumble.

Authelia stands behind him, shaking her head, and mouths, "Hopeless," to me.

Grandma Lula fills a cut glass vase with water, sets it in the middle of the table, and drops the poor wilting dandelions inside. Then she grabs a pitcher of iced tea from the fridge, plunks down some mason jars, and starts filling them.

We all take a seat, since clearly we have been summoned to do so.

"Let's have some biscuits," she says. "There's no harm in a little amelioration."

"Amelior-what?" Quentin says.

"Don't ask." I lean over and whisper in his ear. "I'll

explain this all later."

Grandma Lula serves our biscuits with a jar of Mama's gooseberry jam, and then she opens her bottomless purse and rummages inside.

"My own mother, Celestine, passed this on to me," she says. "I've kept it ever since."

She whips out a crumpled, yellowed piece of paper. It's torn, with about a quarter of the bottom missing. Gingerly, she smoothes the paper flat. Water stains smudge the faded, brownish ink of handwriting.

"What is it?" Authelia breathes.

Grandma Lula slides the paper closer to us. It feels like a dead leaf, and I'm afraid to breathe too hard on it.

CALAMONDIN-MOONLIGHT MARMALADE

My masterpiece. A bittersweet marmalade of utmost power. To guarantee success in preserving, the ingredients must be chosen with care and caution. This marmalade should be cooked in a standard kettle or cauldron lined with porcelain. Willow firewood is recommended. Never stir with an iron utensil; a dogwood spoon is preferred.

There's a long, long list of ingredients that I only half-recognize.

CALAMONDINS, UNBLEMISHED AND WHOLE

MOONLIGHT

SUCRE NOIR

BLESSED WATER

SASSAFRAS ROOT

DRAGON'S BLOOD, FRESH OR DRIED

WINGS OF A 13-YEAR CICADA

A GENEROUS HELPING OF—

I grimace. "I can't even read the last ingredient—it got torn in half. What *is* this?"

Grandma Lula's eyes sparkle with dark secrets. "A page ripped from Shaula's grimoire. A page which was clutched in her hand when they found her dead. A page which contains most—but not all—of a recipe to banish the Ravenous One."

FOURTEEN

I suck in my breath. "Why didn't Shaula tell me she had this?"

Grandma Lula shrugs. "A voodoo spirit as old as her, well, her memory's pretty tattered by now. I'm surprised she's remembered as much as she's told you." She shuts her eyes and tilts her head back. "Now calamondins and moonlight, that's for body and mind. Sucre noir must be for spirit, and blessed water for soul. I'm not too sure about the rest of the ingredients, but Celestine swore this was Shaula's great secret."

"What's sucre noir?" I say. "Is that like film noir?"

Grandma Lula cracks open one eye. "Forgot your French, child? *Noir* means black."

"Of course." My cheeks heat. "So it's black sugar."

She nods. "Black sugar comes in real handy for strengthening a witch's spirit. Keeps you from getting too distracted by voodoo spirits. Some of them like to trick you into feeling so discouraged you give up and go home."

"What on earth are calamondins?" I say.

"Oh!" Authelia pipes up. "That's a kind of fruit, like a tiny orange. My uncle brought some from his travels in the Philippines."

I frown. "We're not exactly in the Philippines."

Authelia waves my comment away. "My uncle shipped in baby calamondin trees so Mother could grow them in our greenhouse. They have fruits on them pretty much all year round, though they are too tart for my tastes."

"That should do the trick," Grandma Lula says. "We won't need many."

"And how about the sassafras root?" I say. "The dragon's blood? The cicada wings?"

Quentin clears his throat. "Excuse me," he says, "but are there *dragons*?"

"Of course not," Grandma Lula says. "There aren't enough mountains round these parts. Besides, dragon's blood is a figure of speech. It's a bright red sap that bleeds out of a pine tree. Greek witches discovered it a long time ago."

"How rare is dragon's blood?" I ask.

"Rare." Grandma Lula purses her lips. "But I have an idea of where we might get some. Down in Louisiana, we have *les marchands de magique*, the merchants of magic. Men who peddle conjure ingredients to witches."

"Like an ice cream truck man?" I say. "Like… Aloysius?"

Grandma Lula's eyebrows shoot up. "I take it the two of you have met?"

I nod. "He sold me some full moon butter."

Quentin and Authelia share a wide-eyed glance, clearly impressed.

"Well then!" Grandma Lula climbs creakily to her feet. "Let's find Aloysius." She glances at Quentin and Authelia. "Breakfast is over, you two. Time for you to finish up those buttermilk biscuits and head on home."

"But what about the calamondins?" Authelia says.

Grandma Lula shrugs. "We can stop by your mother's greenhouse later."

Authelia frowns. "You can't just waltz in there. But I have the key." She pushes her chair from the table and stands. "I'm coming."

Quentin stands, too, his face stubborn. "And I know where to find that cicada's wing."

Grandma Lula sighs and glances at me. "Josephine? I guess you have an entourage."

Flash climbs to his feet and yawns noisily, then slimes my hand with his tongue. I can't stop myself from grinning.

***

Noonday sun soaks my head as we hunt around town. Grandma Lula insists on walking, since she says that's a sure fire way to find an ice cream truck. Authelia kicks off her toe-pinching shoes and tiptoes on the hot pavement in her socks. Behind us, Quentin and Flash pad alongside, both too bashful to look at me.

I'm just about ready to give up and baby my blisters when Authelia gasps.

"What is it?" I say, expecting another zombie.

"I hear it!" She spins around, her face pink. "It's 'Turkey in the Straw.'"

Flash perks his ears and stares into the distance—in the completely opposite direction.

Quentin listens for a second. "It must be coming this way."

I cup my hands to my ears and strain to hear. The twinkling melody meanders its way over the trees and picket fences, followed by the familiar vanilla-white ice cream truck with Aloysius smiling behind the steering wheel.

He waves at us, then stops short. "Alula Bellerose?" he shouts. "Is that you?"

Grandma Lula squints at him in the shimmering heat. "Drive closer! I don't want to walk another mile in this weather."

Never mind that this weather is positively cool compared to Louisiana.

Aloysius nods and drives the ice cream truck nearer. He hurries to turn off the music, sweating, and gives us a nervous grin. "What brings you up north? I was afraid I'd never lay eyes on you again, Alula!"

"Humph," Grandma Lula says. "I planned to keep in touch."

"Josephine! "Aloysius says. "I see you brought your friends. You hungry for ice cream?"

Quentin nods, his face lobster red. "I'd love a—"

"No ice cream," Grandma Lula interrupts. "This is business. You got any dragon's blood on you, Aloysius? Or sassafras root?"

Aloysius scrunches up his face in a smile. "Just the dragon's blood."

He climbs into the back, rummages around, and returns with a tiny tin of ground cloves. "These ain't cloves," he says. "That's—"

"Camouflage, I know," Grandma Lula says.

Aloysius fumbles with the tin, clearly flustered, and hands it to her. "Don't you worry, this is top quality dragon's blood."

"I'll be the judge of that." Grandma Lula peers into the tin, takes a deep whiff, and nods.

Aloysius clears his throat. "That'll be—"

"A dollar fifty." Grandma Lula snaps open her purse. "That's the going rate."

I sneak a smile at Aloysius to encourage him.

He swallows, his Adam's apple bobbing. "Well, dragon's blood has gotten a bit scarcer... but I'd be willing to sell it to you for a song if you might be interested in having lunch with me some day soon?" He meets her gaze.

Grandma Lula looks levelly at him. "Make it dinner," she says, "and it's a deal."

Aloysius nods solemnly and takes her dollar and two quarters, but as soon as Grandma Lula looks away, he breaks into a grin.

We all wave goodbye and walk away.

"Grandma Lula!" I whisper. "You *like* him, don't you?"

"It's a shame about that sassafras root," she mutters, but there's a bit of a blush in her cheeks. "We'll have to dig some up ourselves."

"Flash can help!" Quentin says brightly, oblivious to the flirting that just occurred.

The greyhound cocks his head.

"How so?" I say.

Quentin fishes around in his pocket. "I've got some old sassafras in here somewhere... ta-da!" He pulls out a lint-encrusted hard candy.

"How vile," Authelia says, with supreme disgust. "Were you going to *eat* that?"

"Why not?" Quentin kneels and holds out the candy to his dog. "Here, Flash! Go get it!"

I sigh, waiting for Flash to swallow the candy, but to my surprise the greyhound starts sniffing the dirt and trotting down the road. He stops, circles around, sniffs harder, then breaks into a lope. We all hurry after him.

"Sassafras!" Grandma Lula says, pointing her arm like a weathervane.

Sure enough, there's a big old tree by the side of the road, its three-fingered leaves fluttering in the wind. Flash bounds toward the sassafras and starts digging in the dirt. I fall to my knees beside him and paw at the crumbling earth with my hands. My fingernails scrape a twisted root, and a tingle of conjure darts through me.

"I found one," I say, as the others stand behind me.

I yank the root from the ground and break it from the sassafras tree. It's plump and smells sweet like root beer. Grandma Lula takes it from me, and nods.

I climb to my feet and dust off my knees. "Now how about those calamondins?"

***

Evening sighs over Paris in a smoke-scented wind. A chorus of katydids and crickets sings out among the trees. Me and Grandma Lula stand watch by an old cauldron—one of Mama's, from the attic—while we wait for moonrise. Burning willow boughs crackle and spit underneath the iron belly of the cauldron.

Authelia perches on the picnic bench nearby, polishing and re-polishing the calamondins like they're made out of gold. They do *look* like gold, shiny little orange fruits as big as candies. Next to her, Quentin inspects the contents of a cigar box—his bug collection, which contains the 13-year cicada we need for its wings.

"Could we use some other bug?" he says.

"No," I say.

Quentin sighs dramatically. "But the cicada is my prize specimen."

"That'll do just fine," Grandma Lula says. "Unless you want the Ravenous One to turn you into a zombie instead."

Quentin shakes his head fast, having been explained the situation only an hour ago.

I double-check the conjure supplies clustered on the table. I found a gallon jug of blessed water hidden in Mama's cabinets, alongside an ancient sea-glass jar that rustles with a quart of sucre noir crystals. I hope it's enough.

"Here she comes," Grandma Lula says.

For a moment I think she means Shaula, but then I look up into the sky. The moon rises like a slice of cantaloupe above broccoli trees.

I meet my grandmother's eyes, and I know that it's time to start cooking.

I hoist the jug of blessed water to my hip and pour it into the cauldron. It glugs inside and splashes against the porcelain, sparkling with its own light. The tiny hairs on my arms prickle, though I'm not sure much has happened yet.

"The sugar next," Grandma Lula says.

I pop the cork from the quart of sucre noir. Black crystals glitter like jet gemstones. The sugar slides into the blessed water real easy, melting, turning the water the color of the night sky. I stir the mixture with a dogwood twig, since I couldn't find a spoon, and feel the conjure flowing from my heart, down my arm, and out my fingertips.

Grandma Lula stands in the shadows. "The fruits."

Authelia hands me the calamondins, her face pale, her hair gleaming. She looks like an airy ghost in the moonlight. I zest the calamondins' peels with a paring knife, remembering how I saw Mama do it before with oranges.

She's lying inside in her bedroom right now, so quiet...

No. I can't think about that now. I have to focus on cooking.

With a shaking hand, I drop the calamondin peels into the cauldron. I clench the naked fruits in my fist and squeeze out their juice, letting it trickle down my fingers and mingle with my magic. My arms are starting to ache.

"Save the seeds and pulp," Grandma Lula says. "They have a lot of good pectin in them."

"Pectin?" Quentin says.

"To make the marmalade stick together," she says.

Grandma Lula hands me a muslin bag, and I put all the leftover bits of the calamondins inside. I tighten the drawstring and drop the bag into the cauldron. Golden light swirls in a glowing whirlpool and ripples toward the rim.

"In all honesty," Grandma Lula says, "I ain't sure what goes in next."

"Oh?" I roll my shoulders, which ache with pain. "What order are they written in?"

"That won't work. The recipe was ripped from her grimoire, so the paper is... dead. There's no telling what it should be."

"Sassafras root, dragon's blood, cicada wings," I mutter to myself.

Which should I add next? The order of things is important to conjure, but I only have my intuition to guide me. Sweat slicks my forehead, and I wipe it away, my bones like lead. My stomach flutters with jitters.

I walk to the picnic table and stare at the ingredients. My palm down, I wave my hand over them, slowly, like I'm a divining rod. I let out my breath in a slow whoosh. Conjure tickles my fingertips. Stronger... weaker... strongest. The blood, the root, the wings. I gingerly take the cicada and pluck off its shimmering gossamer wings.

"I know what I want," I say, trying to sound confident.

I crumble the wings over the cauldron, and they rain down in a glitter. The marmalade flares like a firework and changes color from orange to glowworm green. Next, I cup the dragon's blood in my hand and blow the bright red powder into the cauldron. The marmalade plops and goops before darkening into emerald. Last, I take the sassafras and whittle off slivers of the sweet root into the cauldron. The marmalade hisses and shivers, scattering sparks, then settles down into a gorgeous honey-amber.

I pick up the dogwood twig, my body moving slow, as if I'm in a dream.

In a way, I don't feel like I'm Josephine anymore, like I'm standing outside myself and watching myself cook this conjure. My strange hands grasp the dogwood and stir the marmalade twice counterclockwise, twice clockwise. A cloud slides across the face of the moon, and the shimmering marmalade darkens.

"What about the last ingredient?" I say. "A generous helping of…?"

"There's no way of knowing," Grandma Lula says, her eyes dark. "You'll have to add that mysterious ingredient at the very end."

I meet her eyes. "Will that work?"

"Sure," she says. "I dump last-minute conjure into my preserves all the time. Trouble is, the rest of that recipe is in Shaula's grimoire."

A shudder crawls down my spine, and I toss the twig into the fire. "In the swamp?"

"Yes." A shadow passes over Grandma Lula's face.

"That's where we're going next."

***

Mama's bed sags where I sit on the edge.

"I'm going to Louisiana soon," I say. "Really soon. Grandma Lula needs me to come, and I don't know when we're coming back."

I don't even know if she can hear me, but just in case, I keep talking.

"Grandma Lula wants to start driving soon, so I don't think I'm going to get any sleep. We're bringing my grimoire, and the calamondin-moonlight marmalade. In a jar, of course." I laugh feebly. "The cauldron's too big."

Mama's eyelids flicker, and she sucks in a ragged breath.

"Mama?" I gasp.

"*Josephine*," she whispers.

She clenches my hand, then goes limp again, her breathing back to normal. I stare at her, my heart hammering. I scoot away from her and let her hand fall from mine. Her fingernails left crescents where they bit into my skin.

"Mama?" I say again.

Nothing. She's sleeping peacefully.

I take a shaky breath and climb to my feet. Was that good or bad? I don't even know. I'm afraid to touch her again, as horrible as it sounds.

At the bottom of the stairs, Authelia stops me. "Goodbye, Josephine."

I stand there awkwardly, not knowing what to say or do. "You're heading home?"

"Yes, and I'd better get there before Mother or Father finds me missing. Not that they're very good at checking." She gives me a flippant little laugh, but her eyes are scared. "Don't do anything dumb, okay?"

"What," I say wryly, "worried about me?"

Authelia rolls her eyes and shakes her head, then buttons up her coat and heads for the door. I hold the screen door open for her and wave goodbye. She waves back, then breaks into a jog, her shoes clip-clopping on the road.

Quentin follows me out onto the front porch. "Hope a zombie doesn't get her."

I give him a look. "They eat cake, you know."

"They still sound pretty scary," he says, trying out a smile.

I shrug. "You missed the one in the Higgledy-Piggledy. When Mama... you know."

"Ah," he says, looking everywhere but me.

Flash trots over, his head held low, and noses my hand with a whimper. I rub his velvet ears, and he licks me on the knee.

"Well," Quentin says with a tiny smile, "it's getting late.

So late it's early."

I nod and swallow hard.

He hesitates, then touches my hand. "Are you okay?"

I shake my head, and for some reason his fingers on mine make it impossible to hold back my tears any longer. I stare straight at the ground and clench my jaw. Big fat teardrops roll down my nose and plop on the porch.

Quentin hugs me. I lean against him and cry until I don't feel like crying anymore.

"I'm sorry," I say. "I got snot on your shirt."

"It's Josephine snot," he says. "I like Josephine snot."

I laugh, a good hard laugh, which seems a bit crazy considering the circumstances. "Do you hate me now? Because I fed you conjure?"

"Of course not." His voice hums through me. "And don't take all the credit."

I pull back to look at him, and he hands me a handkerchief. I blow my nose as an excuse to think about what he just said. Flash leans on my legs, his long body warm against me. I fold the handkerchief and pat the greyhound on the head.

"So the conjure must have worn off by now," I say, trying to sound casual.

"Sure think so," Quentin says.

I take a shuddery breath. "That's good."

We're both silent for a moment that takes forever.

I lift the Crackerjack charm from under my shirt and

give a wobbly smile to the cute little yellow cockatiel. "You don't want this back?"

"Nope," Quentin says. "Maybe it will bring you some good luck."

My smile widens. "I could use some of that."

"I'd better say goodbye," he says, his voice husky. "May I?"

I look up into his blue eyes, and they tell me what I need to know. My heart flutters in my chest like a trapped bird, until I nod, and finally set it free. He brushes his lips against mine, barely a touch at all, and I lean closer to make it real.

My first kiss. His first kiss, too, since he never was good at keeping secrets.

"I always liked you," he whispers, "more than I wanted to admit."

"Wimp," I whisper back.

He smiles. "Goodbye, Josephine. Come back in one piece."

"I will," I say, and I promise to myself that I'll make it come true.

FIFTEEN

It's that purple time between late night and early morning, when stars and birds meet each other in the sky. I huddle in the front seat of the Fireflite, waiting for Grandma Lula, and listen to the sleepy peeping of a robin in the woods.

Grandma Lula tromps out the front door. "Are you ready, child?"

I clutch the jar of calamondin-moonlight marmalade in my lap, and twist around to make sure my grimoire is in the back seat. "Yes."

Grandma Lula twists the key in the ignition, and the convertible rumbles to life. It's strange without Mama behind the wheel. She backs out of the driveway, gravel crackling beneath the tires like Rice Krispies. I imagine myself sitting at the breakfast table with a giant bowl of cereal, spoon in hand, ready to dig in.

"Eat your eggs!" Mama would tell me. "That cereal's nothing but air."

I shut my eyes, trying to keep the stinging from becoming tears. I let the humming of tires on road fill my ears, glad for such an ordinary sound. I've had enough of zombies moaning and voodoo spirits whispering my name.

"Why don't you rest awhile, child?" Grandma Lula says. "You've been up all night."

"Good idea," I murmur.

Sleep creeps up on me, soft as a cat stalking a mouse, then pounces and takes me away.

By the time I blink myself awake, it's morning, and we're not in Missouri anymore. We're in some sort of podunk middle-of-nowhere town with a diner, a bar, and a church. My grandma parks between two motorcycles outside the bar.

I cover my yawn with my hand. "Where are we? What time is it?"

"Arkansas." She unbuckles her seat belt. "Breakfast time."

"Grandma Lula?" I stare at the tough bikers leaning outside the bar. One of them grins at me, flashing a golden tooth. "You know I'm only twelve, right?"

"Of course I do," Grandma Lula says. "Here, give me that marmalade."

I hand her the jar, and she squirrels it away in her purse.

"Are we eating breakfast in that *bar*?" I whisper loudly.

"Lord, no!" Grandma Lula heaves herself out of the car. "You see that space outside the diner? That one space? It's not big enough for a clown car. Your mother would never forgive me if I so much as scratched this convertible of hers."

Thinking about Mama, even for a second, makes my throat tighten.

"Besides," Grandma Lula says, sauntering past the bikers, "that bar looks skanky."

I heave a sigh and hurry after her.

The diner looks nice enough for Arkansas, with shiny chrome sides outside and red-vinyl booth seats inside. Grandma Lula settles down in a corner and pats the seat next to her. I scoot in beside her, my legs sticking to the vinyl, and wish I hadn't worn such a short dress. Then again, we are going to be rooting around in a swamp.

A red-haired waitress comes by, and we order two milkshakes.

"Milkshakes for breakfast!" Grandma Lula says, with a fake smile. "My treat."

"Wonder how these stack up against Carl and Earl's," I mutter to myself.

Grandma Lula slides her strawberry banana milkshake her way and slurps through her straw. I slide my chocolate one up and take a sip.

"So," she says, "who's that cute boy I saw you kissing?"

I splutter and fumble with the milkshake, splattering my shirt. "Grandma Lula!"

She smiles smugly. "Is he your boyfriend?"

My face turns about as hot as lava. "I'd better get myself cleaned up. Excuse me."

"Mmm-hmm," Grandma Lula says, still smiling.

I grab a paper napkin and hurry to the ladies' room. I head over to the sinks and trickle some water onto my napkin.

"Josephine."

I gasp, my heart pounding. In the warped bathroom mirror, Shaula steps into view. She looks faded and smudgy around the edges, like somebody tried to rub out an inkstain. As I look at her, the stars on her skin start winking out.

"The lighting tree," she whispers.

"What does that mean?" I say.

Shaula grows dimmer and dimmer. "Look… under… the lightning tree."

And she's gone.

I march right back out of that bathroom and over to Grandma Lula. "Shaula was here."

She sucks hard on her straw. "In the bathroom?"

"Yes. She told me to look under the lightning tree."

Grandma Lula pushes aside her milkshake. "Sure hope I'm right. Otherwise we're going to be in a world of trouble."

"Right about what?"

Grandma Lula gives me a meaningful look. "What's in that swamp."

I sip my milkshake too fast, and wince at the headache. "Shaula's grimoire, right?"

"Let's just pray that's all we find."

Now I'm wincing at more than just the cold.

We order some Arkansas cheeseburgers. They taste decent, I guess, though of course I'm still loyal to Carl and Earl's. They haven't got anything like Daddy's limited-time super-special giant onion rings. I scarf my burger in a few bites so we can leave faster, even though Grandma Lula glares at my bad manners.

Finally, we hit the road.

Grandma Lula lowers the Fireflite's convertible top and puts on sunglasses. We cruise down south, the wind whistling by my ears. I lean back and let the coolness wash over my sweaty skin, lulling me into laziness.

"When will we get there?" I say.

"In eight more hours, give or take," Grandma Lula says.

The burger in my stomach starts churning. "I hope Mama's going to be all right."

"Don't waste time worrying."

"Not like I can do much else," I mutter.

Grandma Lula silences me with a stare. "You can pray."

***

One long, long drive later, with evening sky above us, we make it to southern Louisiana.

"New Orleans." Grandma Lula sighs with satisfaction. "*Bienvenue.*"

We cruise through air so muggy we might as well be boating. Grandma Lula eases the car down a tight street flanked by townhouses in shades of cantaloupe, lemon meringue, watermelon, and lime. Ferns pop like green fireworks in pots hanging from the arches of lacy iron balconies. Kids dart between tourists, their flip-flops slapping the sidewalk. Cooking smells braid on the breeze —garlic, seafood, red pepper, and sausage.

My stomach growls. "Something smells good."

"You hungry?" Grandma Lula says. "How do you feel about jambalaya?"

"I love jambalaya!"

"Good. See? We're in the French Quarter. Best jambalaya in the world."

Grandma Lula talks like we're on a vacation, just having fun, but I can see a tightness in the way she holds her mouth.

I keep my voice light. "Anything wrong?"

"Nothing," she says. "Yet."

A spidery shiver crawls down my spine. I watch the sun dip down into the Mississippi and melt into puddles of gold.

Grandma Lula parallel parks on the street, and we walk two blocks to the Café Enchanté, a little restaurant in a beautiful old brick building. Night-blooming jasmine perfumes the breeze. Inside the Café Enchanté, electric candles wink in low chandeliers. Our waiter reminds me of Daddy, with the same twinkly blue eyes.

"*Bonsoir.*" He smiles at me when we take a seat. "You look thirsty. Something to drink?"

I hesitate, and Grandma Lula says, "Iced tea, *s'il vous plait. Merci.*"

Hearing all this French in a Louisiana accent, I can't help but think of Shaula. I fidget on the edge of my seat, my tailbone sore from the long drive. Or maybe I'm just antsy because I can see a clock from here, time ticking away.

Grandma Lula rummages in her bottomless purse. "I got your grimoire from the car."

I swallow hard, my mouth dry. "What for?"

"You'll see."

She drops my grimoire onto the table. It thuds like it's a lot heavier than it should be. I slide it toward me and open it a crack, peeking at the pages. Words swim sleepily on the paper, then start to wiggle more when they see me.

If they can see me.

"This was Celestine's most secret of secrets," Grandma Lula says.

She lays a tiny cloth-bound book on the table. The

gilded letters on the cover have almost been rubbed off, but I can still tell that it's a book of prayers. She opens the book of prayers and tugs out a pressed piece of paper.

"Here." Grandma Lula slips the paper toward me. "Look."

Gently, I take the paper and spread it flat. It's tattered and thin, covered with ink splotches and odd scribbles. It smells musty.

"That's a map," Grandma Lula says. "Celestine drew it when she was your age, back in 1880, so she wouldn't ever forget where she lost her mama out there in the swamp. But that map has been ruined for as long as I can remember."

I squint at the map. Some of the splotches look like they might be trees, and that zigzag could be coastline. "Wait, so this shows where Shaula passed on? Did you have this the last time we looked for her grimoire? I don't remember it."

"Yes," Grandma Lula says, "but it was scarcely any help at all."

The handsome waiter comes by with our iced tea, and we smile innocently at him.

"Are you two ladies ready to order?" he says.

Grandma Lula doesn't even look at the menu. "We'll both have the jambalaya."

"Excellent choice." He whisks our menus away, and Celestine's map flutters to the floor. "Sorry, let me get that for you."

I wince as he picks up the map, afraid it's going to crumble into a thousand pieces.

Grandma Lula purses her lips and waits until the waiter leaves. "Be quick and copy that map down before there's no map left to copy!"

"Copy?"

"In your grimoire, of course." Grandma Lula hands me a ballpoint pen.

"Sure thing," I say.

I flip to a blank page in my grimoire and start sketching Celestine's map. Too bad I'm not an artist. And the curious words in my grimoire don't seem to be helping. They nibble at the edges of my drawing before the ink has even dried.

Shaula's words whisper in my ear. *The lightning tree.*

I squint at a splotch on Celestine's map, trying to figure out if it's a tree or a mountain. Apparently she wasn't much of an artist either. I wonder if the only talent in my family is conjure, and there isn't room for anything else.

I decide it's a tree—a lighting tree, split in half by a thunderstorm—and jot it down.

Grandma Lula peers at the map. "That should do."

I hand Celestine's map back to her, then watch the map in my grimoire darken.

She leans back in her chair and sips her iced tea. "New Orleans is a capitol of conjure. Some say it's *the* capitol.

Marie Laveau and her daughter, the most famous Voodoo Queens, lie buried not more than a few blocks from here. Just think, they once walked these streets in all their finery, inspiring awe in the eyes of any who saw them."

"How long ago was that?" I press the cold glass of my iced tea to my forehead.

"Over eighty years ago."

I stare into a flickering electric candle. "Wouldn't it be something if Shaula met them?"

Grandma Lula's eyes look faraway. "The veil between the living and the dead is thin here. Do you know why all the graves here are aboveground, child? The water's too close under the dirt for people to be buried properly."

I wonder where Shaula might be buried, then shudder. The swamp, of course.

Our waiter brings us two bowls of jambalaya, a jumble of shrimp, sausage, veggies, and rice. My mouth waters something fierce. I pop a big spoonful into my mouth. Chili pepper fire burns across my tongue and all the way down my throat.

"Good?" Grandma Lula says.

I give her something between a wince and a smile.

She bursts out laughing. "Good lord, Josephine. You forgot about jambalaya."

"No, I didn't!" I wheeze, and swig some water. "This is just… extra hot."

"Your tongue got wimpy up in Missouri."

"Mama cooks spicy food all the time." I eat another spoonful of jambalaya to prove it.

Grandma Lula's laugher turns into a strangled gasp. She stares straight over my shoulder.

I twist around to look, my eyes still weepy from the peppers. A woman stands silhouetted in the doorway of the Café Enchanté.

Mama.

I nearly choke on my mouthful of jambalaya. Mama drifts into the Café Enchanté. A stylish red dress swishes at her ankles, and she pats her up-do to make sure it's still in place. She's wearing more makeup than normal.

"Mama?" I say, my voice hoarse.

"That can't be Clara," Grandma Lula says.

The handsome blue-eyed waiter meets Mama at the door, and she says something to him. He nods, then leads us to our table.

"Josephine!" Mama sounds bubbly. "Grandma Lula! I've been looking for you."

My stomach sours. "You're supposed to be in Missouri."

"Oh?" Mama arches an eyebrow. "While you two have all the fun?"

"You were... sick."

"Well, I feel fine now." Mama winks at me. "Scoot over and let me sit."

Winks? Mama *never* winks. The sour feeling in my stomach grows into full-blown nausea. I stare straight at her face, but she won't look at me. She's wearing an awful lot of perfume, something else not right.

"Clara?" Grandma Lula sips her iced tea slowly. "How did you get here?"

"I borrowed Laurent's truck." Mama slides a chair over and slithers in. "I'm *famished*."

There's a hiss in her words, a sizzle like oil on a hot grill. My heartbeat thuds rapid-fire in my chest. I push my chair back from the table, and it scrapes on the floor with a horrible screech. Mama glances at me, her eyes dark, too dark.

"You're not her," I whisper.

Mama takes a sip from my iced tea. She licks the rim of the glass like she's tasting it. "I'm sorry, I didn't catch that."

Grandma Lula grabs my hand under the table and gives it a hard squeeze. "Josephine."

I grit my teeth. "You're not Mama."

The handsome waiter comes by with a pitcher of iced tea. "Anything else I can get you?"

Mama unfolds her legs and stands, her eyes locked on mine. "Nothing on your menu." She laughs, a crackling sound like burning wood.

"Give Mama back." I leap to my feet. "Give her back now!"

"Josephine," Mama sighs, "I'm enjoying this body far too much to leave."

I clench my fists by my sides and wish for instant conjure, for a spell that will kick out the Ravenous One right here, right now. Instead, I grab the pitcher of iced tea from the waiter and toss it into Mama's face. She gasps and throws up her arms, but tea drenches her from head to toe. Ice cubes clatter on the floor.

Mama stands there panting, wrings some tea from her skirt, and looks at me.

"Josephine...?" she mumbles, confusion in her eyes.

"Mama?" I suck in my breath, and touch my fingers to her wrist. "I'm sorry, I—"

"Don't touch her!" Grandma Lula rises to her feet and grabs me by the elbow all in one movement. "She's still possessed!"

Mama's skin burns like a hot iron skillet under my fingers. Inside her eyes, the hunger of the Ravenous One rekindles. A wind starts to whip around us, tangling my curls in my face, tossing the skirt of Mama's red dress. The electric candles in the chandeliers burn bright, too bright, then shatter with the smell of lightning.

"*Josephine,*" hisses the Ravenous One.

The Café Enchanté plunges into darkness. Everybody in the restaurant screams, without even knowing they should be so, so much more afraid.

I find Grandma Lula in the darkness, latch onto her hand, and we sprint headlong through the Café Enchanté, the Ravenous One looming so close behind me I can almost taste his terrible stink in my mouth. I press my lips together tight.

"Outside!" Grandma Lula commands.

We burst through the doors on the restaurant and skid out onto the sidewalk. I almost crash into a big man with a big camera, and he spits a nasty word. I don't bother telling him there's something much nastier coming. The Ravenous One saunters through the doors wearing Mama's soaking wet body. His fire burns in her eyes, spilling out and shining across her face. The big man starts snapping photos. I keep running.

Grandma Lula pants beside me, her heels clacking on the pavement. "Sweet Jesus!"

"Almost there," I say. "I see the Fireflite."

We leap into the convertible, slam the doors, and start driving. In the rearview mirror, I see Mama walking down the street, lopsided with one broken high-heel. Shuffling like a zombie. Did the Ravenous One leave her undead?

Some tourists meander across the street, and Grandma Lula taps the horn.

"Come on," she says. "We've got to get to the swamp before it's too late."

I glance back at Mama. She shucks her shoes and follows us barefoot. I exhale hard.

Not a zombie. Not yet.

We break free of the French Quarter crowd, gain some speed, and leave behind both Mama and the glittering nighttime New Orleans. Moonlight glows through muggy fog steaming from the earth, and through thick moss cobwebbing all of the oak trees. The convertible's tires rumble over pavement cracked like black alligator skin.

A shudder passes over me, and feverish heat prickles my skin.

"Josephine?" Grandma Lula says. "Are you all right?"

I frown. "I feel sort of hot."

"You shouldn't have touched Clara."

"I thought maybe the Ravenous One had left Mama."

Grandma Lula laughs hollowly. "A pitcher of iced tea ain't going to stop a voodoo spirit that powerful any time soon!"

I blow out my breath. "What will?"

"Shaula's marmalade."

"Yes, but *how*?"

"You eat it, of course!" Grandma Lula flares her nostrils, a vehement look in her eyes. "Think for a moment about the ingredients. Those calamondins will give you strength of body, the moonlight strength of mind, and of course the blessed water is there to keep your soul in one piece long enough to fight the Ravenous One."

"But it didn't work!" I try not to shout. "Shaula ate it, and she died."

Grandma Lula face hardens. "Celestine told me Shaula summoned the Ravenous One."

My heartbeat stumbles. "She *summoned* him? Why?"

"Because she knew how close she was to banishing him. She wasn't strong enough." She fixes me with a fierce stare. "But you are."

"Me?" My throat tightens, and my voice cracks. "Why does it have to be me?"

"Because he's after you, Josephine."

"Of course." I take a ragged breath. "So after I eat the marmalade, then what?"

"You banish the Ravenous One," she says simply.

I grit my teeth. "That's not very helpful."

"The Ravenous One is an abomination." Grandma Lula's fingers tighten on the steering wheel. "He shouldn't even be here, not like this. Back in the beginning he was nothing more than Hunger. We witches knew him as Papa Nom, and still pray to him as such. But that was before he learned to love the taste of a witch's soul."

I shiver, wondering what it feels like to have your soul sucked out. All hollow inside?

I think for a moment. "But Shaula said he has all the conjure of all the witches he's ever eaten. How can my conjure beat his?"

Grandma Lula looks at me. "This isn't a battle of conjure. This is a battle of wills."

SIXTEEN

Tree branches tangle so thick overhead that only slivers of moonlight slip though. The green murky smell of swamp fills my nose. Peeping, chirping, rasping songs press against my ears—frogs and crickets and who knows what else. I stand close to our car's headlights, waiting for Grandma Lula, my grimoire under one arm.

"Knew we'd need these," she says.

Grandma Lula plops a pair of rubber boots on the road. I kick off my shoes and pull on the boots, my feet already sweaty, but that could be nerves more than anything. The headlights go out, and I jump, my heart pounding.

"That was me," Grandma Lula says, and she flicks on a flashlight.

"Lord, you almost gave me a heart attack!" I say.

"Uh-huh. Now let's see that grimoire of yours."

I lay my grimoire on the still-warm hood of the Fireflite

and flip it open. In the circle the flashlight makes, words dart around the paper like scared fish. I turn the pages until I reach my copy of Celestine Leroy's map of the swamp.

"It's different," I say, scarcely even surprised at this point.

"Of course it is." Grandma Lula points to the corner of the map. "We're closer now. See? We're on that levee right there. And there's that lightning tree Shaula told you about. We just have to walk due northwest for a way."

"How long is a way?"

She shrugs. "Better start walking. Wait."

Grandma Lula rummages in her purse and pulls out the jar of marmalade, a silver teaspoon, and a crystal vial with a tiny cork. She pops out the cork with her thumbnail and spoons a teaspoon of marmalade inside.

"That should do the trick," she says, "if I lose my purse in this swamp."

She sounds matter-of-fact, but I know she's not worried about her purse. I take the vial of marmalade. It's wrapped in wire, so I thread it into my necklace. It slides down and clinks beside the yellow cockatiel charm that Quentin gave me.

"Perfect," Grandma Lula says.

I shut my grimoire and hold it tight. I follow Grandma Lula into the swamp, and she follows her flashlight's beam into the darkness. Under my feet, grass turns into mud, and mud turns into soupy muck. My boots squelch so loud I'm sure all the gators for miles around will hear me. And the Ravenous One, for that matter.

"Stop!" Grandma Lula says. "The grimoire?"

I hand it to her, and she hands me the flashlight. She opens the book to the map, and frowns. It looks like we're on the edge of the water. And across from us, there's the lightning tree, standing in the middle of blank paper.

"Those boots won't be enough," Grandma Lula says. "See?"

I shine the flashlight across the water. An ancient cypress tree grows straight out of the swamp, its bark blackened to charcoal by some long-ago fire. No, not fire. Lightning. A shudder passes over me, and my eyelids flinch shut.

"Josephine?" Grandma Lula grabs my elbow. "You all right?"

"Feel a little funny," I say.

There's a tight, throbbing feeling inside my skull, like the start of a headache, and the skin on my fingertips prickles.

"It's Shaula's grimoire," she whispers. "Either that, the Ravenous One is close."

I open my eyes, and circle around like a human compass. The prickling in my fingertips gets stronger whenever I face the lightning tree.

"The grimoire," I say. "I hope."

Grandma Lula glances at my own grimoire. The map ripples like the moon's reflection in the water. "This won't be much use to us anymore. You're going to have to go out there yourself and find Shaula's grimoire."

"Figures." I kick off my boots and hand the flashlight to her. "Shine that for me."

"Feel for the conjure. Use your gift."

"If you watch out for gators," I say, echoing my words from four years ago.

Barefoot, I wade into the swamp. Lukewarm water ripples and tugs at my ankles, inviting me to sink. I hold my arms out at my sides and let my hands graze the surface. Prickling climbs up my fingers, cold and hot, like icy fire.

Conjure. Raw conjure, and lots of it, leaking out of Shaula's grimoire.

I wade in farther. Water rises to my knees, then my waist. Goosebumps speckle my skin. My headache sharpens into panging pain in my skull. I glance up at the shawls of Spanish moss, and they sway in a wind I can't feel.

Like a bomb went off, a ripple of magic surges through the water, stealing my breath away and knocking me off my feet.

A wave sweeps toward me, like an echo of a memory. I bob in the water.

"Josephine?" Grandma Lula calls. "Find anything?"

"Not yet," I say. "I need to go deeper."

I kick off from the ground and swim toward the lightning tree. Cool swamp water sweeps over me like silk. I touch the cypress's trunk, and a bright sparkling rush of conjure dances up my arm. I gulp a deep breath, dive into the pitch-black water, and grope blindly for the grimoire. My fingers slide over cypress roots, rocks, and a smooth rectangle half-buried in the mud. Conjure pours, tingling, over my hand.

Shaula's grimoire. It has to be.

I swim to the surface, gulp more air, and dive down again. I wedge my fingernails beneath the rectangle and try to pry it out, but it's caught in the cypress roots. I struggle underwater, my lungs burning, and the rectangle yanks free.

I rise from the swamp with it clutched in my hands, and raise it to the moonlight.

A leather-bound book, untouched by the water, with a title in unknown words. In the air, the conjure doesn't feel as strong, but it's still there, tickling over my fingers like electric spiders. I twist in the water, the book held high, to show Grandma Lula. She shines her flashlight straight at me, and I wince, blinded by the light.

"I can't see!" I shout.

She lowers her flashlight. "What is that? Is that it?"

"I think so! I think I found Shaula's grim—"

A hand closes around my ankle, and yanks me underwater in one swift jerk.

I barely have time to suck in air before my head plunges underwater. I clutch the grimoire in my hand like it's a life preserver, but of course it isn't, and I'm sinking into the swamp. I kick hard, and the hand lets go of my ankle.

A light floats toward me. Grandma Lula's flashlight? Did she jump in after me?

You ain't going to drown.

I see the shape a woman, swimming closer, glowing around the edges like a ghost. Mama. Her eyes burn with the light of the Ravenous One. I can see her face so clearly, see how she smiles and mouths one word. *Josephine.*

My lungs on fire, I float in the water and stare into her burning eyes.

She reaches for me, her fingers drifting toward my face. Her smile widens, and she bares her teeth in a hideous grin.

Stars sparkle before my eyes. Shaula glows into being between us.

Swim, Josephine! Swim!

Her words burn into my mind like a firebrand. My legs jolt into life, and I swing them hard, rising toward the surface, Shaula's grimoire still clutched in my hand. I rise from the darkness and suck in a ragged gasp.

"Josephine!" Grandma Lula says. "Jesus, what happened?"

"Stay back," I gasp, my throat raw. "Don't come any closer."

She shines her flashlight on the water. Ripples widen around me, and bubbles rise from the bottom of the swamp. Mama's swimming back up, and the Ravenous One's coming to get me. I can't let him hurt her, or Grandma Lula.

I have to lure him to me.

Newfound strength steels my muscles, and I swim away from the bank, shutting out the sound of Grandma Lula's yelling. The grimoire seems to grow heavier and heavier in my hand, but I don't dare let it go. My arms brush up against mud, and I grab a handful of grass to haul myself out onto land. Panting, I perch on the edge of the bank, balance Shaula's grimoire on my knees, and pry the mysteriously dry book open.

I can see words, smudged and scribbled, but it's too dark to read them.

"Don't you dare touch my granddaughter!" Grandma Lula shouts into the blackness.

"The light!" I shout back. "Give me some light!"

She points the flashlight my way, and the thin beam travels across the swamp and lands on the rest of the ripped page in Shaula's grimoire.

LUCK

A generous helping of luck.

That's it? That's the last ingredient for the marmalade? I flip through the pages frantically, but they're either blank or blurred ink.

"Grandma Lula!" I scream across the water. "It's luck! The last ingredient is luck!"

She screams something back, but I can't hear her words.

I fumble for the vial of marmalade at my neck, and my curls tangle with the chain. I yank on the chain, and it snaps in two. The vial zips down the broken chain, but the yellow cockatiel charm stops it from falling into the swamp.

My fingers are shaking so bad I can't grab the cork. I bite it with my teeth and spit it out.

Water ripples by my feet, and Mama rises from the swamp, her eyes on fire with hunger. She crawls up onto the ground, her red dress waterlogged and ruined. The Ravenous One uses her mouth to laugh. I scramble back, clutching the grimoire, but there's nothing against my back but tree roots and mud and—

I shake the marmalade onto my tongue and swallow the bittersweet conjure.

Darkness spills from Mama's mouth. The Ravenous One rises from her body and twists over me, a tangle of tentacles. He sweeps around me with a rush of stinking heat, and I find myself staring straight into his fiery eyes.

Josephine, he sighs. *At last, you're mine.*

I gasp and swallow a mouthful of voodoo spirit. The Ravenous One creeps through my lungs and into my blood and—

Josephine!

Not the Ravenous One's voice. Shaula's?

You are strong. You can control Hunger.

Before I can figure out what she means, everything goes black.

***

Emptiness gnaws in my stomach. The delicious taste of conjure sweetens my mouth, but I'm still not satisfied. I look down at the witch whose soul I have just devoured. She lies in the mud, her eyes closed like she's only sleeping.

That girl. She's...

I swat that thought like a mosquito, then turn toward an old witch who's shining a light at me and screaming. Her soul must taste good.

Grandma Lula.

I fly over the swamp and reach out with my tentacles. She grabs a jar of marmalade from her purse, but that isn't enough to stop me.

That girl. She was Josephine.

The old witch unscrews the jar, but I soar high above

her and—

I'm Josephine.

It's me. I'm inside of the Ravenous One. I'm floating inside his darkness like a bird caught in a thunderstorm.

"No!"

The word hisses from my mouth in a wind of scorching heat. Grandma Lula flinches back, raising her arm to shield her eyes. I wrench myself backward, yanking my tentacles away from her, and retreat over the water. I can feel the Ravenous One fighting me, but I'm not going to let him have Grandma Lula.

I glance back, and see my human body lying in the mud. Empty of my soul.

Whispers tickle my thoughts. *Who are you?* says one voice. *Are you Shaula's?* says another. *You're a strong one, darling.* All the souls of all the witches the Ravenous One has ever devoured, echoes of themselves, alone until now.

"Let them go," I say.

The Ravenous One tries to scream, and a moan escapes his mouth—*my* mouth. I'm in charge now. On the shore, Grandma Lula stares up at us, her face blank. The Ravenous One strains against me, struggling to reach her.

"You're Hunger," I say. "Nothing more."

Inside me, all the witches devoured by the Ravenous One crowd together, quivering with fear and hope. I open my mouth wide and breathe out. Glittering souls spill from me and rise into the heavens, as bright as constellation of stars. Their light winks and flashes in the waters of the swamp, and it's so pretty I laugh.

"Josephine," Grandma Lula whispers, her eyes gleaming with reflected souls.

I feel a little yanking in my belly, and then I rise into the star-spangled sky.

SEVENTEEN

"Josephine." Somebody shakes my shoulders, and I wince. My head feels like an elephant sat on it. "Josephine, wake up!"

Slowly, my thoughts click into place. "Grandma Lula?"

I crack open my eyes, and wonder why there are so many stars out on a night like this. I sit up too fast, and my vision blurs.

"Careful!" Grandma Lula helps me up. "You just came back."

"Back?" I rub my forehead. "Ouch."

"Ouch? *Ouch*?" Her fingernails dig into my shoulders. "Child, you were dead for a good five minutes! It took me that long to coax your soul back into your body. I think you liked floating around with those witches a little too much."

Then I notice the tears gleaming on her cheeks, and I

remember that the stars are souls.

"The Ravenous One! Is he—?"

"Gone." Grandma Lula's grip eases up a bit. "He disappeared when you left him."

"And Mama! Is she—?"

"She's right here." She gives me a wobbly smile. "She's sleeping."

I crawl on my hands and knees over to Mama. She's lying on the grass, one arm flung up under her head, a faint smile on her face.

I reach for Mama, then hesitate. "She's not a zombie?"

Grandma Lula shakes her head. "The Ravenous One left her in peace."

I lay down beside Mama and give her a hug, never mind that there's squishy swamp mud beneath my cheek. Above us, the souls of the witches zip like shooting stars, traveling their separate ways in the world now that they're free.

Free. I suck in a shuddery breath. After who knows how many years.

"*Bonsoir*, ladies."

Shaula strolls from the swamp like it's something she does everyday. Who knows, maybe she does. She smiles at Grandma Lula, who looks dumbstruck, then walks to me. I sit upright, and can't help but notice I'm caked in stinky mud and duckweed while Shaula looks spotless. I guess there are some benefits to being a spirit.

"Are you leaving?" I ask, and suddenly there's a lump in my throat.

Shaula stares at the horizon, where the shooting stars fall. "If only I could."

"You turned yourself into a spirit." Grandma Lula talks in a low voice. "There's some powerful dark conjure keeping you here."

Shaula meets her gaze, and the two witches stare at each other for a long moment.

"You're right," Shaula says, "granddaughter."

Grandma Lula narrows her eyes slightly. "I never met you. Before, I mean."

"I know. I wish you had."

I rise to my feet. "Please don't fight." My eyes sting. "You're family."

Shaula smiles, a sad smile, and it makes her even more beautiful. "Oh, Josephine. Look at us standing here. Four generations of witches, each one of us more stubborn than the last. If only Celestine could have been with us."

Grandma Lula reaches out to Shaula's arm, but there's not enough there to touch.

Shaula looks to me. "And I knew you were the strongest of all, Josephine."

Grandma Lula tilts her head. "That's what *I've* been saying this whole time."

"You both did." I laugh, and somehow it brings me closer to crying.

"Josephine," Shaula says, "could you bring my grimoire to me?"

I nod, and look around. We're still standing on the island with the lightning tree. I glance at Grandma Lula, who's only muddy up to her knees. "How did you get here, Grandma Lula? You don't look nearly as wet as me."

"It's not an island," she says. "It's a peninsula."

I sigh. "We could have used a better map."

"My apologies," Shaula says. "The Ravenous One would not let me come sooner."

I hunt around in the grass and cypress roots, then find Shaula's grimoire. It's still in one piece, even after I got possessed by the Ravenous One.

Or after I possessed him, I guess. That seems more like it.

"Burn it," Shaula says.

"What?" Grandma Lula looks sharply at her. "What a waste of conjure!"

"It was my grimoire." Shaula's face stays unreadable. "I won't be needing it anymore."

"But..." Grandma Lula trails off. "Well, let's see if I can't conjure up some fire."

By "conjure up," she means grabbing some matches from her bottomless purse. I set Shaula's grimoire on a log, then strike a match.

I glance at Shaula. "Are you sure?"

"Yes. Quick, before that match burns out!"

My hand trembling a bit, I inch the flame closer to the edge of the grimoire.

"Wait," Grandma Lula says.

The match sizzles out with a curlicue of smoke.

"Shaula," Grandma Lula says, "shouldn't you be passing these recipes down?"

"I thought you didn't like dark conjure," I say.

Shaula arches an eyebrow. "What Josephine said."

"You're wrong." Grandma Lula plants her hands on her hips. "There's a time and a place for dark conjure. It's just more dangerous."

"Yes," Shaula says. "Dangerous. Burn it, Josephine."

I strike another match, and before I can chicken out, I let the flames creep over Shaula's grimoire. It catches on fire real quick, and crackles green and purple in the blaze. The bittersweet smell of conjure rises in the smoke and tingles in my nose. I breathe in deep, trying to bottle up that smell inside me for another day. Shaula's eyes glimmer in the firelight as she watches her life's work crumble to embers and ashes.

"Now your grimoire," Shaula says.

"What!" I squawk. "I'm not going to—"

"No." Shaula steadies me with a feather-light hand on my shoulder. "Open your grimoire on that log over there, *ma chère*."

I do as she says, glancing at her suspiciously.

"Now take the ashes," she says, "and sprinkle them into

your grimoire."

I scoop the ashes into the palm of my hand, then brush them onto my grimoire. Where the ash touches the paper, it turns into tiny gray words. Tiny baby words, which wiggle away to hide in the crack between the pages.

Grandma Lula sucks in her breath. "Did you…?"

"My grimoire's secrets belong to Josephine now." Shaula's eyes look so dark and clear. "I couldn't think of a better witch to have them."

***

Shaula says goodbye at the edge of the swamp, not forever, just for now.

In a darkness edged by dawn, we drive northbound to Missouri. Mama stirs when we stop at a gas station, revived by the aroma of cheap coffee.

"Lord," she says, blinking herself awake. "Laurent, what *is* that awful smell?"

"Mama!" I lean across as far as my seatbelt will go, and hug her. "You're awake."

"Did you make coffee?" she says blearily. "Is that why it smells so bad?"

"No, Clara," Grandma Lula says, "blame it on a gas station in Louisiana."

"Louisiana?" Mama jolts one-hundred percent awake. "But—we were just in the Higgledy-Piggledy. Weren't we?"

She doesn't remember anything. I guess that's a good thing?

"It's a long story," I say.

"Well, you'd better tell me right now!"

I grin at the no-nonsense sassiness in her voice.

"Well," Grandma Lula says, "you might have gotten yourself a little bit possessed."

"A little bit?" Mama narrows her eyes. "There's no such thing!"

Grandma Lula gives her a meaningful glance in the rearview mirror, and Mama listens to the rest of the story without saying a word.

Finally, Mama looks at me and exhales like she'd been holding her breath. "Josephine?"

"What, Mama?"

"I was wrong about you." She smiles at me, her eyes tearing up. "And thank heavens!"

I see Grandma Lula roll her eyes in the rearview mirror.

Mama's face gets all hard again. "But don't you ever sneak off and play with dark conjure like that without telling me, you hear?"

"Yes, Mama," I say, though I'm not sure how I'm going to keep that from happening!

***

By the time we get back to Missouri, the zombie curse has broken. Daddy tells us that the Ralstons' barn was full of some very confused Society ladies and one postmaster who was considerably less crabby than usual. Horton knocked on our door looking for answers, bramble scratches on his arms and a bit of frosting on his shirt. Luckily, Daddy calmed everybody down and invited them inside for lunch.

Strangely enough, nobody was hungry for cake.

While Mama talks to Daddy upstairs, and Grandma Lula whips up lunch, I help Cleon serve our guests some hot get-well-soon tea. They all sit in the dining room, basking in the morning sun and blinking a lot.

"Does this mean they're un-undead?" Cleon whispers in my ear.

"Cleon!" I whisper back.

Mrs. Bourbon squints at us, still looking pretty dazed, but always eager to eavesdrop on possible gossip. Beside her, Mr. Glumphy keeps giving me little nervous glances and dabbing his face with a napkin, though there's no cake left.

I force myself to smile at Mr. Glumphy. "Tea?"

He twists the napkin in his fingers. "I'm... I'm not that hungry."

"You mean thirsty?" I say.

He swallows hard, his Adam's apple bobbing, and looks at the teapot. "Is that," he whispers, "the voodoo kind?"

"The *good* voodoo kind," I say. "To make you better."

Mrs. Chantecler bonks him on the knee with her purse, which she dragged around the entire time she was a zombie. "Oh, just drink it!"

Mr. Glumphy pales. "You're a witch, too, aren't you?"

"Not a very good one," she says, with a sweet smile.

I suspect Mr. Glumphy thinks she means *evil*, because he turns even whiter. He takes the mug I offer him, slurps some tea, and winces.

"It's peppermint, not dog pee," Mrs. Chantecler snaps. "And say thank you!"

"Yes ma'am!" He looks at me, and mumbles, "Thank you, miss."

I resist the urge to laugh.

Outside the dining room window, the magnolia tree's branches wave in a breeze. Beckoning me. I excuse myself and carry a teacup with me, but I don't sip a drop. Our clay statue of Papa Nom smiles up at me.

I kneel in the grass. "Hello, Papa Nom," I whisper. "I hope you're okay."

I trickle the tea over him so he can drink it, then close my eyes and say a silent prayer.

"Josephine! You're back!"

I leap up, my heartbeat galloping, and find myself face-to-face with Quentin and Flash. "Sweet Jesus! Why do you keep sneaking up on me in my own backyard? Don't you ever use the doorbell? We have a doorbell, you—"

He sweeps me into his arms and plants a kiss on my lips.

I pull back, laughing. "You're horrible!"

Quentin pretends to look hurt. Flash dances between us, wagging his tail so hard he keeps whipping my legs with it. I crouch to hug the greyhound, and he gives me a much wetter kiss on my cheek. I grimace, then laugh.

"So you did it?" Quentin says. "The Ravenous One is gone?"

"He is!" I say. "Well, I *am* talking to you right now."

He points to my teacup. "Why did you dump that?"

I shake my head. "I didn't dump it. I gave it to Papa Nom." I wave my hand at the little statue. "He's the spirit of Hunger."

Quentin smiles. "And Thirst?"

"I guess so? I'd have to ask Mama." I reach into my pocket and pull out the yellow cockatiel charm. "Thanks again for this. It *was* lucky."

"Oh?" he says. "What happened?"

"Long story," I say, "but without it, I would have lost everything in the swamp."

He sobers. "Does... does this mean you're a witch? For real?"

I nod, and lift my head a little higher. "I'm helping Mama with the family bakery. Of course, it's going to be tough selling conjure in Paris after all this. Mama says we're going to need a sprinkling of trustworthiness in every bite."

Quentin shrugs. "McArthur Mills got blamed for the zombies. It was in the news."

"Really?"

"Yes. Conjure in their cheesecake."

I snort. "You mean crappy ripped-off conjure."

"And I heard through the grapevine that Authelia ratted them out."

I break into a grin. "I was wondering what she'd do about that."

Quentin smiles at me, that shy sort of smile, then darts in for another kiss. I dodge him and dance away, laughing. Flash barks.

"Don't you distract me!" I say. "I've got to get back inside."

"Okay," Quentin says, his cheeks pink. "Can I ring your doorbell and join you?"

"Sure thing," I say.

He salutes me and jogs away. Flash sprints past him, about ten times faster.

I sigh and shake my head. As I walk around the house, movement in a window catches my eye. Shaula strolls into view among the rustling reflected forest. Her white dress ripples behind her, like she's almost here with me.

"Busy with your beau?" she says.

I freeze in my tracks, my face burning. "What? No."

Lord, is everyone going to tease me about Quentin?

Shaula laughs, and her voice drops to a lullaby croon. "Then you should have the time to meet me tonight, by the magnolia tree."

"Why?" I say, though I'm pretty sure I know the answer.

"You have only had a taste of conjure, Josephine. There is so much more to explore."

Who knows what recipes she slipped into my grimoire?

"Tonight?" A tingle zips down my spine. "I'd better start cooking."

ABOUT THE AUTHOR

K. L. Kincy (Kirkland, Washington) loves zombies, though she hopes to meet only the cake-eating kind. *Deadly Delicious* is her first book for children. She has a BA in Linguistics and Literature from The Evergreen State College.

K. L. Kincy also writes for teens and adults as Karen Kincy.

Find her online at:

www.karenkincy.com

www.facebook.com/deadlydelicious

CPSIA information can be obtained at www.ICGtesting.com
Printed in the USA
LVOW12s2314050415

433413LV00004B/227/P